TERRIFYING
TOYS
OF
TENNESSEE

Here's what readers from around the country are saying about Johnathan Rand's *AMERICAN CHILLERS:*

"I just read Terrible Tractors of Texas, and it was great! I live in Texas, and that book totally freaked me out!"

-Sean P., age 9, Texas

"I love your books! Can you make more so I can read them?"

-Alexis B., age 8, Michigan

"Last week, two kids in the library got into a fight over one of your books. But I don't remember what book it was."

-Kylee R., age 9, Nebraska

"I read The Haunted Schoolhouse in three days, and I'm reading it again! What a great book."

-Craig F., age 12, Florida

"I got Invisible Iguanas of Illinois for my birthday, and it's awesome! Write another one about Illinois!"

-Nick L., age 11, Illinois

"My brother says you're afraid of the dark, which is silly. But my brother makes things up a lot. I love your books, though!"

-Hope S., age 9, California

"I love your books! Make a book and put my name in it. That would be sweet!"

-Mark P., age 10, Montana

"I'm writing to tell you that THE MICHIGAN MEGA-MONSTERS was the scariest book I've ever read!"
                                    -Clare H., age 11, Michigan

"In class, we read FLORIDA FOG PHANTOMS. I had never read your books before, but now I'm going to read all of them!"
                                    -Clark D., age 8, North Carolina

"Our school library has all of your books, but they're always checked out. I have to wait two weeks to get OGRES OF OHIO. Can't you do something about that?"
                                    -Abigail W., age 12, Minnesota

"When we visited Chillermania!, me and my brother met you! Do you remember? I had a red shirt on. Anyway, I bought DINOSAURS DESTROY DETROIT. It was great!"
                                    -Carrie R., age 12, Ohio

"For school, we have to write to our favorite author. So I'm writing to you. If I get a letter back, my teacher says I can read it to the class. Can you send me a letter back? Not a long one, though. P.S. Everyone in my school loves your books!"
                                    -Jim A., age 9, Arizona

"I LOVE AMERICAN CHILLERS!"
                                    -Cassidy H., age 8, Missouri

"My mom is freaked out by the cover of POISONOUS PYTHONS PARALYZE PENNSYLVANIA. I told her if she really wanted to get freaked out, read the book! It's so scary I had to sleep with the light on!"
                                    -Ally K., age 12, Tennessee

"Your books give me the chills! I really, really love them, but I don't know what one I like best."

-Jeff M., age 12, Utah

"I was read WISCONSIN WEREWOLVES, and now I'm freaked out, because I live in Wisconsin. I never knew we had werewolves."

-Angie T., age 9, Wisconsin

"I have every single AMERICAN CHILLER except VIRTUAL VAMPIRES OF VERMONT. I love all of them!"

-Cole H., age 11, Michigan

"The lady at the bookstore told me I should read NEBRASKA NIGHTCRAWLERS, so I did. I just finished it, and it was GREAT!"

-Stephen S., age 8, Oklahoma

"SOUTH CAROLINA SEA CREATURES is the best book in the whole world!"

-Ashlee L, age 11, Georgia

"I read your books every night!"

-Aaron. W, age 10, New York

"I love your books! When I read AMERICAN CHILLERS, it's like I'm part of the story!"

-Leroy N., age 8, Rhode Island

"KREEPY KLOWNS OF KALAMAZOO is my favorite. It was awesome! I did a book report about it, and I got an 'A'!

-Samantha T., age 10, Illinois

AMERICA's #1 SERIES FOR MAXIMUM CHILLS!

#21: Terrifying Toys of Tennessee

Johnathan Rand

An AudioCraft Publishing, Inc. book

Book storage and warehouses provided by Chillermania!©
Indian River, Michigan

Warehouse security provided by:
Lily Munster and Scooby-Boo

American Chillers #21: Terrifying Toys of Tennessee
ISBN 13-digit: 978-1-893699-92-2

Librarians/Media Specialists:
PCIP/MARC records available at www.americanchillers.com

Cover illustration by Dwayne Harris
Cover layout and design by Sue Harring

Printed in USA

TERRIFYING
TOYS
OF
TENNESSEE

VISIT CHILLERMANIA!

WORLD HEADQUARTERS FOR BOOKS BY JOHNATHAN RAND!

CHILLERMANIA!

**I-75 Exit 313
then south
1 mile!**

Visit the HOME for books by Johnathan Rand! Featuring books, hats, shirts, bookmarks and other cool stuff not available anywhere else in the world! Plus, watch the American Chillers website for news of special events and signings at *CHILLERMANIA!* with author Johnathan Rand! Located in northern lower Michigan, on I-75! Take exit 313 . . . then south 1 mile! For more info, call (231) 238-0338. And be afraid! Be veeeery afraaaaaaiiiid . . . .

The building sat vacant for years.

It was old, and there was a 'For Sale' sign in the window that looked as if it had been placed there a long time ago. The windows were dirty and grease-stained. My friends and I never paid much attention to the building; we'd pass it on our way to school, but we had no reason to give it any more notice than a casual glance. It was on Southeast Broad Street, sandwiched between *Captain Whipple's Famous Ice Cream* store on the left and *Lost Soles*, a second-hand shoe store, on the right. Dad said the old building used to be a hardware store. But that was years ago, and I never remember it being anything more than an old building in its final stages of disrepair. I suppose every city has a building like it, and I figured that one of these days someone would tear it down and start fresh. Maybe they would construct a new building and open a clothing store, or perhaps a book store.

I was wrong on both counts. The building wasn't torn down, and what opened in its place wasn't a clothing store. It wasn't a book store or a hardware store. It wasn't a restaurant or a deli or a dollar store.

It was a *toy* store.

Now, I have to admit, I was surprised. I thought the building would probably end up being torn down. But I thought a toy store would be really cool, especially if it wasn't just a toy store for little kids. I've been in some toy stores that have really cool things like model rockets and airplanes, games . . . all kinds of different toys. Maybe the new toy store would be like that. I hoped so.

My name is Eric Carter, and I live in Murfreesboro, Tennessee. I was born in Nashville,

but we moved when I was very little. I've always liked it here. I like the people; I like the weather. I like my school and my teachers. I like my family. Oh, sure, sometimes my little sister, Madeline, really bugs me. She's four, and sometimes, she's a pest. But as far as little sisters go, she's pretty cool.

What I *don't* like are toys. Not anymore. Not since what happened at the toy store. But to understand everything, I have to start at the very beginning . . . the day something very strange happened when I walked by the old, decaying building downtown.

The day began like any other. It was summer, and it was hot. That's one thing you can count on in Murfreesboro, Tennessee: if it's summer, the weather is going to be steamy. I don't mind at all. Summer is my favorite time of the year.

I got up and went into the kitchen for a bowl of cereal. Madeline was already awake and out of bed. Still in her pajamas, she was sprawled out on her belly in the living room, watching cartoons on television. When she's watching cartoons, it's nearly *impossible* to get her attention. I think the house could fall down around her, and she wouldn't notice. Unless, of course, she couldn't see the television.

While I was eating my bowl of cereal, Dad came into the room. He's a mechanic for a car dealership in Murfreesboro, and he was wearing his dark blue pants and blue shirt with his name embroidered on it. My dad's name is Richard, but everyone at the dealership calls him 'Wizard' because he can fix almost any car. I know it sounds like I'm bragging, but my dad really is *that* good when it comes to fixing cars. His friends are always bringing their cars over to our house when they're having trouble with them.

"Hey, Big E," he said, ruffling my hair with his hands. That's what Mom and Dad call me: Big E. They've called me that ever since I can remember. They don't call me that *all* the time, but a lot.

"Hey, Dad," I said.

"What's up today?" he asked.

"Me and Mark and Shayleen are going fishing," I said. "It should be a good day for it."

Mark Bruder and Shayleen Mills are friends that live on our block. Shayleen and I will be going into fifth grade at Hobgood Elementary this year;

Mark will be going into fourth. We fish in a small ravine not far from where we live. Actually, it's only a small pond, and very few people know about it. But there are lots of fish in it, including some big ones.

"Well, bring home a couple of big fish for dinner," Dad said. "I'll see you tonight."

"See ya," I said.

Dad turned to the living room and looked at Madeline on the floor. "See you tonight, little lady," he said. Madeline just stared at the television. She was so engrossed in cartoons that she didn't even hear him. Like I said: when she's watching television, it's almost impossible to get her attention.

After Dad left, I returned to my bedroom, got out of my pajamas, and put on shorts and a T-shirt. When I returned to the kitchen, Mom was there.

"Did you get some breakfast?" she asked.

"Yeah," I replied. "I had some cereal. Can I go fishing with Mark and Shayleen today?"

"I don't see why not," Mom said, "but there's something I'd like you to do for me, first."

I hope it's not the windows, I thought. Earlier in the week, Mom had mentioned she wanted me to clean all the house windows, inside and out. It's not a really hard job, but it takes a long time.

"Can you run down to the store and get me a few things?" Mom asked.

Cool, I thought. *That'll be easy.*

"Sure," I said.

Mom scribbled a short list on a yellow piece of paper and handed it to me, along with some money.

"And I want change back," Mom said. "Don't spend it on candy, like you did last time."

"I won't," I said. "I'll be right back."

I was glad Mom asked me to run to the store, instead of asking me to clean the windows. That would have taken a couple of hours, while going to the store would only take fifteen minutes.

I left our house and walked across the lawn. The grass was shiny and wet with dew. The sun was burning brightly, and the morning was already very warm. Sprinklers sprayed water onto glistening green lawns. Hidden birds called out from trees. It was going to be a great day.

I walked up the block and rounded the corner. Soon, I was downtown walking along busy Southeast Broad Street. Like most mornings, it was filled with cars and trucks as people drove to work.

And I don't know how or why the old building caught my eye. I'd passed it a million times before, and I hardly ever paid attention to it. It always looked the same.

Today, however, something had changed. I noticed it right away, but I couldn't put my finger on just what was different.

I stopped walking and gazed at the dilapidated building. Traffic hummed behind me on the street, and I heard the tired sigh of a truck's air brakes.

Something is different, I thought. *What is it?*

I stared for a moment, until I finally realized something: the sign in the window of the old building had changed. For as long as I could remember, there had been a dirty yellow *For Sale* sign in the window. The sign itself was every bit as grimy as the building.

Now, the *For Sale* sign was gone. In its place

was a brand new sign, all shiny and colorful. I was too far away to read it, so I walked over to the building and stopped. I gazed at the sign.

Opening Soon! it read, in big, red letters. *Maxwell's House of Terrific Toys! The finest, most wonderful toys in the entire world! Strange and magical toys and games! You name it, Maxwell's got it!*

Beneath the words were cartoons of various toys: a Jack-in-the-Box, a rag doll with red hair made of yarn, a model airplane, and a train.

"A toy store!" I said out loud. "That'll be *awesome!*"

And I really *was* excited. Not only was it going to be a new toy store, but it would be close to my house! I could go to the store any time I wanted!

I re-read the sign in disbelief. My mind was whirling, and I was so focused on the sign that I didn't even see the huge reflection of a monster in the window . . . until the thing was already upon me.

By the time I saw the reflection in the window, the thing was already lunging for me. I spun around to dodge the attack, but it was too late. Mark Bruder had already wrapped his hands around my waist.

"Gotcha!" he exclaimed as he squeezed once, then let go.

I turned and looked at his reflection in the glass. Because the window was so old and dirty, it made his reflection appear to be something it wasn't. In fact, Mark's reflection was much larger than he actually was. It had really freaked me out.

"You got me, all right," I said, and I pointed to his reflection in the window. "Look at yourself

21

in the glass. You look like an ogre."

"Hey, that's cool!" Mark said, raising his arms in the air. His reflection in the glass looked really crazy, like he was ten feet tall!

"Ready to go fishing?" he asked as he dropped his arms to his sides.

"Yeah," I said, "but I've got to run to the store for my mom, first."

"I just saw Shayleen," Mark replied. "She's got to clean her room. I told her to come over to my house in an hour, and we can head to the pond from there. Can you make it?"

"I'll be there," I said. Then, I pointed at the window. "Did you see the new sign?" I asked.

Mark nodded. "I saw it last night! A toy store will be sweet!"

"For sure," I said. "I hope it opens soon."

We said good-bye to each other, and I started walking. I thought about the new toy store. *When will it open?* I wondered. *What kind of toys will be there?* The sign said there would be all kinds of toys from around the world. It would be exciting just to walk through and see them all.

And I'd been saving money all summer. I do

odd jobs around the neighborhood: mowing lawns, raking, things like that. I even opened up a savings account at the bank. Every month they send me a letter in the mail called a 'statement.' The statement told me how much money I had in my bank account. So far, I'd earned almost forty dollars since school ended.

After getting the items Mom needed from the grocery store, I started walking home. Mom didn't really need a whole lot, and everything fit into a single, brown paper grocery bag that I carried with one arm.

As I passed by the old hardware store, I again looked at the sign and wondered when the toy store would open. Maybe it was written on the sign, and I missed it when I'd read it earlier.

So, I walked up to the window and read the sign again, looking for something that would indicate when the grand opening would be.

Nothing.

I took a step to the left and looked at my reflection in the old glass. In the window, my form was distorted and large, and I remembered how freaked I'd been when Mark had surprised me.

And it occurred to me then, that in all the years of walking by the old building, I'd never looked in any of the windows, and I had no clue what was inside the crumbling building. I had no reason to.

Now, however, I was curious.

I took a step closer and gazed through the filmy, grease-stained glass.

The building was empty, except for one very strange thing: in the center of the old store stood a doll. She had dark brown, curly hair with two blue ribbons tied in it. Her dress was also blue, and she was wearing matching blue shoes.

But, what was so horrifying was the fact that the doll was *moving!* Her eyes were blinking, and her mouth was moving up and down! I couldn't be positive, but it appeared she was staring right at me. I could hear her speak, too, and I leaned toward the window and listened.

What I heard her say was nothing less than terrifying.

"Eric," the doll was repeating, over and over again. *"Eric . . . Eric . . . Eric . . . ."*

My eyes bulged, and my jaw dropped. My

arms went limp, and the bag of groceries tumbled to the cement and tore open. Items scattered around my feet, but I didn't even notice them. I was too shocked, too horrified to take my eyes away from the bizarre doll in the middle of the empty store.

"*Eric . . . Eric . . . Eric . . . .*"

A nightmare was coming to life, right before my eyes!

I blinked my eyes several times as my thoughts spun wildly out of control.

How did that doll get there? How did it know my name? In school, we read a book about dolls that came to life in Delaware. I had nightmares after reading it . . . even though it was just a book. I knew it wasn't *real,* but it still creeped me out.

There was nothing else in the building, except for some old shelves covered with a frosting of gray dust. Even the floor was layered with a dirty film of powder.

But in the dust, I could make out a single pair of footprints that led across the floor and vanished into a dark room at the back of the building.

The doll had walked to the center of the room!

It was impossible! The doll had somehow come to life and was now standing in the center of the old hardware store, blinking her eyes at me and calling my name.

"Eric . . . Eric . . . Eric . . . ."

A large form suddenly appeared as a reflection in the window, and I turned around. A woman had been walking along on the sidewalk, and she strode up to me.

"Are you all right?" she asked. She sounded very concerned.

"Yeah," I said, and I suddenly realized I'd dropped the groceries on the ground. The bag had split open, and the things I'd bought for Mom were strewn all around my feet.

"I guess the bag slipped out of my hand," I said, and I knelt down. The woman also knelt down and helped me pick up the groceries. Thankfully, the things I'd bought—some spices, a bag of frozen vegetables, cake mix, a can of ground black pepper, a bag of peanuts, and two red peppers—weren't damaged. It's a good thing I hadn't bought anything in a glass jar. It would've shattered for sure.

"It doesn't look like anything is damaged," the woman said. "Here. The paper bag isn't torn too bad. I think you can still use it."

She handed it to me, and I cradled the bag in one arm. Then, we began piling in the groceries. If I was careful, I would be able to carry the bag home without dropping anything.

"There," she said, after all the groceries were secure in the bag. "That should hold until you get home."

"Thank you," I said.

"What were you looking at, just then?" she asked.

"A doll," I said. "Look."

The woman leaned toward the window, and I turned and peered back inside.

The doll was gone!

Not only was the doll gone, but there was another set of tracks in the dust, coming out from the back room. They led right to where the doll was, then returned to the room in the back of the building!

Suddenly, I felt really foolish. "I . . . I guess I must've just imagined it," I said to the woman.

"Well, be careful with your groceries on the way home," she said. Then, she walked away.

I continued staring into the store through the grimy glass.

What's going on here? I wondered. *Where did that doll come from? Where did she go? How—and why—was she calling my name?*

And so, I decided something right then and there. I decided I would take the groceries home to Mom. Then, since I still had time before I had to meet Mark and Shayleen, I would come back to the old hardware store to see if I could find anything out. Of course, I couldn't go inside, but maybe if I looked around in the back, behind the building, I would find a logical explanation for what I had just experienced.

After all: dolls really can't *talk*. They can only speak words they're programmed to say.

Still, the doll's voice haunted me. I could still hear her words in my head as she repeated my name over and over.

Eric . . . Eric . . . Eric . . . .

I walked away, and I never saw the eyes that were watching me the whole time.

When I got home, Madeline was still lying on the floor in front of the television. She was watching a purple dinosaur sing songs and dance . . . the same one I had watched when I was her age. I really liked him when I was little.

I carried the groceries into the kitchen. Mom was busy making something. I could smell all sorts of different scents: chocolate, strawberries, and fresh bread.

"I had a little blowout on the way home," I said as I carefully handed her the torn brown bag containing the groceries. "But you don't have to worry . . . nothing broke or tore open."

"Thank you for going to the store for me," Mom said, and she bent down and kissed my forehead. "You're sweet."

"I know," I said with a smirk. "Hey, guess what?"

"What?" Mom asked as she began putting away the groceries I'd brought home.

"You know that old building downtown?" I said. "The one that's falling apart?"

"You mean the old hardware store?" Mom asked.

"Yeah," I said, nodding. "Well, there's a new sign in the window. It says it's going to be a new toy store! It says it'll be opening soon!"

Mom looked surprised. "Really?" she said. "I thought it was going to be torn down."

"I thought so, too," I said. "But it's not. The sign says the store is going to be called *Maxwell's House of Terrific Toys.*"

"That sounds like a lot of fun," Mom said with a smile. "When will it open?"

I shook my head. "The sign didn't say," I replied. "It just said it would be opening soon. But what was really weird was—"

I caught myself before I finished. *Should I tell Mom about the doll I'd seen?* I wondered. *Probably not. She'd probably think I was losing my mind.*

"What was weird?" Mom prodded.

"Oh, nothing," I said. "I just think it's weird that the old building is going to be turned into a toy store."

"Yeah, that *is* strange," Mom said. "But it's a good thing. It's nice to see someone is going to fix it up."

I looked at the clock on the stove. I had about forty-five minutes before I had to be at Mark's house. I had plenty of time to go back to the old building and poke around for the doll.

"Well, I'm heading out," I said. "We'll be fishing for a couple of hours, I'm sure."

Mom looked down at me and frowned. "Whatever you do," she said, "when you go fishing today, do *not* bring home one of those ugly catfish. You nearly scared me to death last time."

"I won't, Mom," I said. A couple of weeks ago, I caught a huge catfish. He was twenty-two inches long and weighed ten pounds! I'd never caught one that big before, so I took it home to show Mom and Dad. Dad, of course, was at work, and Mom was at a neighbor's with Madeline. Well, when I got home, I realized the bucket I was carrying the catfish in was too small, and he couldn't swim around. So, I filled up the bathtub with water and put the catfish in it. He had lots of room to swim. I even put Madeline's rubber ducky in the tub to keep the fish company. A little while later, I was in the backyard throwing my balsawood glider when I heard a terrible scream. I ran inside to find my mother standing at the bathroom door, pointing to the catfish in the bathtub.

"Young man," she said angrily, "what is this . . . this *thing* doing here?!?!"

"I caught him in the river!" I said. "I wanted to show you and Dad! Isn't he cool-looking?"

Mom was angry. "Don't put live fish in the bathtub!" she scolded. "Get it out, this instant!"

I raced to the garage to get the bucket, so I could get the fish out of the bathtub. Secretly, I thought it was kind of funny that Mom had been so freaked out by a silly catfish. But I really hadn't intended to scare her. Had I known she had come home, I would've ran inside to show her the fish. Although she still might have been mad, it wouldn't have scared her so much. Just remember: if you really want to freak out your mom, put a fish in the bathtub and don't tell her about it.

I hurried out of the house and jogged down the street. In minutes, I was once again in front of the old, decrepit hardware store. I walked up to the dingy window and peered inside.

Nothing had changed. I could clearly see the small footprints the doll had made, and the larger footprints created by what must have been an adult.

I read the sign again.

Opening Soon! Maxwell's House of Terrific Toys! The finest, most wonderful toys in the entire world! Strange and magical toys and games! You name it, Maxwell's got it!

Then, I walked to the left side of the building. There was a thin alley that led to the back. It was empty, except for a couple of steel garbage cans with the words *Captain Whipple's Famous Ice Cream* printed on them.

I decided to go through the alley to the back

of the building. There weren't any 'No Trespassing' signs posted, so I figured there was nothing wrong with using the alley.

I had only taken two steps when I saw her again.

Her.

The doll.

She emerged from the back of the building, and now she was taking stiff, robot-like steps in my direction! Not only that, she began to speak, just like she had done from inside the building!

"Eric . . . Eric . . . Eric . . . ."

I couldn't believe what I was seeing or hearing. The doll kept walking toward me, her movements jerky and uncertain. It was as if she had come to life!

I was so scared I couldn't move. Part of me wanted to turn and run, but I couldn't. My brain commanded my legs to work, but they wouldn't listen. All I could do was stare in horror as the doll came closer and closer.

Then, at the end of the alley, a shadow appeared, and the figure of a man emerged from behind the building.

"Ah!" he exclaimed. "Trying to get away

again, I see!" He started up the alley, toward the doll.

My fear began to subside, but not much. *What did he mean by that?* I wondered.

When the man reached the doll, he picked her up. Then, he looked at me, then back at the doll. "Still not working properly, I see," he said, as if he was speaking to a living, breathing child. Then, he turned and looked at me.

"Hello there, my young friend," he said with a wave of his hand. He walked toward me, carrying the doll beneath his arm. "And how are you on this wonderful summer day, hmm?"

"Fine," I said, staring at the doll beneath his arm. The man was tall, like my dad. He had shiny black hair and a mustache that curled up at each end. He was dressed a little odd, too. He wore shiny yellow pants and a satin red shirt. His shoes were covered with blue sequins. He reminded me of one of those giant lollipops with a multicolored swirl.

"Good, good," the man said. "All boys should be fine during the summer, for summer certainly is a fine time of year, no?"

"Yes, it is," I said, and I was feeling better already. He was obviously a very nice man and very good-natured. I was no longer frightened by the doll he was carrying, but I sure was curious!

"How does that doll walk and talk?" I asked.

The man held out the doll. "You mean Priscilla, here?"

"Yes," I said. "I saw her through the window a little while ago."

"Ah! Yes!" the man said. "I thought that was you. I saw you leave. Watching you from the back room, I was. I had picked up Priscilla and taken her to the back. When I returned to introduce myself, you were already gone. But go on. Tell me what you saw."

I continued. "The doll—Priscilla—was standing in the middle of the room, blinking her eyes and calling my name. And she was calling my name again in the alley when you picked her up just a minute ago."

The man looked puzzled. "Your name?" he said. "And just what is your name?"

"I'm Eric Carter," I said. "The doll was repeating my first name over and over. She was saying *'Eric . . . Eric . . . Eric.'* It kind of freaked me out."

"Well, let's see," the man said. He placed the doll on the ground, and she immediately began walking. "Battery powered, you know," the man said. "Unfortunately, her on/off switch has been malfunctioning." He scratched his head and looked puzzled. "Sometimes, she turns on and off all by herself." Priscilla started to talk as she staggered a few steps.

"Eric . . . Eric . . . Eric . . . ."

"See?" I said. "She's saying my name."

"No, no, no," the man said, shaking his head. "She's not saying your name. You see, she's broken. She's actually supposed to be saying *'Ma-ma, Ma-ma.'* Notice how her mouth isn't opening all the way? There's a part in her jaw that is broken, so she can't speak clearly."

Sure enough, the doll's mouth was only opening part way. Still, it sounded like she was calling my name.

"Eric . . . Eric . . . Eric . . . ."

"When she works properly, she walks and talks. I'm afraid all she does now is stumble forward and try to say *Ma-ma.*"

He picked up the doll again and tucked her beneath his left arm. The doll went silent and stopped moving.

"Well, Mr. Carter," he said as he extended his right hand. I took it in mine, and he shook it firmly. "My name is Maxwell P. Kleagle," he said.

"You're . . . you're the guy that's opening up the toy store!" I exclaimed.

"Quite right, quite right," he said, taking a slight bow. "And what an amazing toy store it will be! Everyone loves toys, do they not?"

I nodded, then I looked at the doll under Mr. Kleagle's arm. "Well," I said, "*most* toys. I don't play with dolls."

"Just as well for a boy of your age," Mr. Kleagle said. "In fact, Priscilla, here, would be better off with a young girl, no? Someone who could care for her? Tell me: do you know of any young ladies who might like her company?"

"You mean Priscilla?" I asked.

"Yes, indeed," the man said. "You see, I just can't seem to make her work right. She's broken, but she's not worthless. However, no one will buy a defective doll. Perhaps you know someone who would like her."

"I have a little sister named Madeline," I said. "She *loves* dolls."

Mr. Kleagle's eyes lit up. His thick, dark hair shined in the morning sun. "Do you think *she* would look after Priscilla?"

"Yeah, she would," I said. "I'll bet my sister would *love* Priscilla!"

Mr. Kleagle held out the doll. "Then, consider this a gift," he said. "Free of charge. Take Priscilla to your sister, as my gesture of goodwill to you, your family, and the city of Murfreesboro. And be sure to let everyone know about my new toy store!"

I took Priscilla in both hands and looked at her. I stared.

"Is something wrong?" Mr. Kleagle asked.

I paused for a moment, staring into the doll's eyes, which almost looked . . . *human.* Even her plastic skin looked real. An eerie feeling crept over me, like the way I feel when I get to a really scary part in a book.

"No, nothing's wrong," I replied. "My sister

will really like her new doll. She's going to be surprised. Thank you."

Mr. Kleagle's face changed. He didn't look mad or mean, but there was something in his expression that made me uncomfortable.

"Oh, she'll be surprised, all right." Then, he let out with a gallon of laughter. "Yes, yes, she'll be surprised. You have a good day, Mr. Carter, and be sure to drop in when my store opens."

Suddenly, he turned and strode back through the alley. He began whistling a tune, something unfamiliar that I couldn't place. I stared after him until he reached the back of the building, turned, and vanished.

I wonder what he meant by that? I thought. It was really strange the way he had said my sister would be surprised.

I looked at Priscilla, and I know this is going to sound crazy, but it sure looked like that silly doll was staring back at me. She somehow looked . . . alive, and it reminded me of that book we read in school. Once again, a really creepy feeling swelled up inside me, and Mr. Kleagle's words echoed in my head.

Oh, she'll be surprised, all right.

That was what he'd said.

Oh, she'll be surprised, all right.

Madeline would be surprised with her new doll, for sure.

But Priscilla had a few surprises of her own . . . surprises Mr. Kleagle hadn't told me about.

To say that Madeline was surprised was the understatement of the year.

She wasn't just *surprised* . . . she went bonkers!

I still had plenty of time before I had to meet up with Mark and Shayleen, so I took the doll home. Madeline hadn't moved an inch. She was still splayed out on the floor in her nightgown, watching television. Some commercial was on, advertising breakfast cereal.

But, before I gave Madeline the doll, there was something I had to do. I flipped Priscilla over. At the base of her neck was a small battery compartment. I popped it open, exposing two red batteries. I took both of them out and put the small lid back on the compartment. I placed the batteries on the coffee table.

There, I thought. *That'll keep Priscilla from going off on her own.*

I tiptoed across the carpet and snuck up behind Madeline. Then, I reached around her and stood Priscilla right in front of her face.

Madeline jumped up, surprised. Then, she sported a grin I thought was going to rupture her cheeks.

"Mine?" she exclaimed.

I nodded. "It's from the guy who's opening a new toy store downtown," I said. "He doesn't want her anymore, but she needs to have a good home."

I don't think I've ever seen my kid sister so excited in her entire life! She grabbed Priscilla and hugged her. "My dolly!" she exclaimed. She kissed the doll's nose. It was actually kind of cute.

"Her name is Priscilla," I said.

"I like that name," Madeline said. "It sounds good."

Then, she turned and ran into the kitchen, carrying Priscilla beneath her arm. The doll's hair bobbed as she ran. It was funny, sort of. Priscilla was nearly as big as my sister!

"Mommy! Mommy!" she cried. "Look at my new dolly!"

I followed her to the kitchen, where Mom was holding the doll and looking at her. She looked confused.

"Where did this come from?" Mom asked.

"The guy that's opening the toy store," I replied. "I just met him. He says Priscilla doesn't work right, and he hasn't been able to get her fixed. So he gave her to me to give to Madeline. It's hers, now."

"Well, that was very nice of him," Mom said. "We'll have to go in and thank him properly, once his store opens."

"I'm going to play in my bedroom with Brazilla," Madeline piped happily.

"No, that's *Priscilla,*" I said. "Not *Brazilla. Priscilla.*" But it didn't really matter what she called the doll. She had already fallen in love with her, and that's all that mattered.

Mom handed Priscilla back to Madeline, and she whisked off to her bedroom with her new doll in tow.

"That was very nice of that man," Mom said, "and you, too. It sure made your sister happy."

Madeline's happiness, however, didn't last long. I was just about to speak when my sister began screaming in her bedroom.

"BRAZILLA BIT ME! BRAZILLA BIT ME!"

I knew all along something was wrong with that doll . . . and now Madeline did, too!

Mom and I sprang from the kitchen, and we raced down the hall to Madeline's bedroom. I was there first, and I pushed her door open.

Madeline was sitting on her bed, crying. Priscilla was laying on a pillow, face down. Her brown hair was splayed out all around her head.

"What happened?!?!" Mom asked as she brushed past me and sat on the bed.

Madeline held up her thumb. There was a tiny droplet of blood near her thumbnail.

"Bra . . . Bra . . . Brazilla b-b-b-bit me!" Madeline stammered.

"Let me see," Mom said. Madeline held out

her thumb, and Mom looked closer. "What were you doing?" she asked.

"I . . . I was . . . I was just holding her," Madeline sniffled. "She bit me!"

Mom picked up the doll. "Where were you holding her?" she asked.

"Right there," Madeline said, pointing to the doll's neck. "I was just hold . . . holding her, and she *bit* me!"

Mom looked closely at the doll. Then, she smiled. "Priscilla didn't *bite* you," she said. "Look here. There's a safety pin that's holding her dress on. It snapped open. You poked yourself on the pin, that's all."

Now that Madeline knew the truth about what had happened, she stopped crying and looked at her thumb. She hadn't hurt herself badly. All she had done was prick her thumb on the safety pin, enough to pierce the skin and draw a tiny droplet of blood.

"I thought she bit me," Madeline said as she stared at her thumb.

"Dolls can't bite people," Mom said. "Now: let's go into the bathroom and get your thumb clean. I don't think you'll even need a bandage."

Mom stood, and Madeline slid off the bed. Mom held Madeline's hand, and they left the bedroom.

Now, I wasn't sure about this at the time, but I thought I heard laughter.

Girl laughter.

Doll laughter.

I was sure I saw Priscilla's leg move, just a tiny bit. At the time, though, I just figured it was my imagination.

Now, I know better.

Priscilla was more than just a doll. Matter of fact, *all* of the toys at *Maxwell's House of Terrific Toys* were more than just toys, as I would soon find out.

And they weren't terrific.

They were *terrifying*.

Later that day:

"What's so strange about a doll?" Mark asked.

The three of us—Mark, Shayleen, and myself—sat close to the pond. We were spaced about fifteen feet apart, so we could cast our lines into the water without getting them tangled. But the fish weren't biting, and none of us had caught anything.

"I guess you'd just have to see her," I replied. "She looks real. She creeps me out."

"If the doll creeps you out, why did you take it to your sister?" Shayleen asked.

"I guess I just thought I was being silly," I replied. "It's just a doll. But still, I was a little freaked out by it. And there's something about that Maxwell guy, too. I mean . . . he seemed nice enough, and all. But I just got a weird feeling after he'd given me the doll to give to Madeline. I felt like he wasn't telling me something. Like he had something to hide or keep secret."

"Hey," Mark said, "if he's giving away free toys, I don't care how weird he is."

"The doll was broken, and that's why he gave it to me to give to my sister," I said. "I'm sure he isn't giving away toys for free. He won't make any money if he does that."

We didn't talk any more about the doll or the toy store for the rest of the day. And we didn't catch very many fish, either. The few we did catch weren't very big, so we threw them back.

So much for fish dinner.

When I got home, Madeline was on the living room floor on her belly, watching television. She'd positioned Priscilla next to her on the carpet, and it looked like the doll was watching television, too. Mom was sitting on the couch, reading a newspaper. She looked up.

"How was fishing?" she asked.

"Not very good," I said. "The only ones we caught were little. Hope you weren't counting on fish for dinner."

Mom smiled. "Your father called from work. He said he's going to pick up a pizza on his way home."

Cool! If there's one thing I love, it's pizza.

After I got cleaned up, the phone rang. Mom answered it, and then she brought it to my room. "For you," she said. "It's Mark."

I took the phone from her and put it to my ear. "Hey," I said. "What's up?"

"Eric?" Mark said. He sounded nervous. "Remember when we were talking about toys earlier today?"

"Yeah," I replied.

"And how you thought the doll that guy gave you was odd?"

"Sure," I said. "What's the matter?"

"I don't know," Mark replied. "Nothing, probably. But . . . well . . . maybe you should just come and look at this."

"Look at what?" I asked. Mark's voice was very strange. I'd never heard him sound like that before. In fact, he sounded—

Scared.

"I'll be right over," I said, and I clicked off the phone.

What's wrong with Mark? I wondered. I took the phone into the kitchen and hung it up. Then, I walked into the living room where Mom had returned to the couch.

"Mom, can I go to Mark's for a couple of minutes?"

Mom turned and looked at the clock on the wall. "Only for a few minutes," she said. "Your father will be home soon."

"I won't be long," I said, and I headed out the door.

What's wrong with Mark? I kept wondering.

I'd know soon enough.

I raced down the block, sprinting on the sidewalk, all the while wondering about Mark's mysterious phone call. I'd never heard him sound that frightened.

It only took me a minute to reach his house. Even before I got there, I could see him standing on the porch, staring down at something. I slowed to a jog, then to a steady walk as I approached.

"What's the matter?" I asked, stopping at his front porch steps.

"*This* is the matter," Mark said, pointing down.

On the porch at his feet was a monkey. Not

a live monkey, of course, but a stuffed monkey. It sat about a foot high, and in each of its paws was a brass cymbal.

"Where did *that* come from?" I asked.

"That's what I want to know," Mark said. "Mom said it was here earlier, when she went to the mailbox. She figured it was mine, and I had left it on the porch."

"Have you ever seen it before?" I asked as I reached down and picked up the monkey.

"That's what's so weird," Mark replied. "When I was little, my grandparents gave me a monkey, just like this one. It was a birthday gift. When you wound him up, his arms moved and he banged his cymbals together. And his eyes flashed red. At first, I thought it was cool . . . but for some reason, it freaked me out. After a while, I *hated* that monkey. One weekend, we had a garage sale, and I sold him for a dollar. I never wanted to see him again."

"Why were you so afraid of him?" I asked, inspecting the monkey in my hand.

Mark shrugged. "I guess it was because I was little, and I had dreams of the thing coming alive. I know it's silly . . . but I was only four or five years old."

I knew how Mark felt. When I was that age, we had a small sculpture of a lion that sat on our coffee table, and I was afraid of it. My dad finally had to put it in the garage. Now, of course, it seemed silly. But when you're little, lots of things can frighten you for no reason at all.

"Well, *someone* had to put this monkey here," I said. "He didn't walk here by himself."

There was a large key coming out of the monkey's back, and I gave it a few turns. Instantly, the monkey began waving his arms, beating the cymbals together. They gave off a tinny, splashing-metal sound. His eyes flashed red, on and off. After a few moments, the monkey stopped moving.

"What are you going to do with it?" I asked.

Mark shook his head. "I don't know. I just don't know where it came from, or how it got here."

I turned the monkey upside down. There was a small white tag attached to the bottom of one of his legs. Something was written on it . . . and when I read what it was, I was shocked.

Mark must've caught my surprised expression. "What?" he asked. "What is it?"

"How long ago did you say your grandparents gave you that monkey?" I asked.

Mark thought for a moment. "Oh, five or six years ago," he replied.

"And you sold it in a garage sale?" I asked.

Mark nodded. "Yeah," he replied. "A long time ago."

I handed the monkey to him and showed him the white tag.

When he read it, he was horrified. The tag read: *To Mark Bruder, on his birthday. Love, Grandma and Grandpa.*

It was the very same monkey Mark had sold years ago! It was unbelievable, but it was true!

"It's impossible!" Mark said. "It's just impossible!"

"Something really weird is going on," I said.

And it was about to get weirder.

A *lot* weirder.

Later that night, in bed:

My eyes were open, and I stared at the shadows on the ceiling. I couldn't sleep. It was almost midnight, but all I could think about was Mark's monkey.

How did it get there? I wondered. *Someone must've placed it there. Why?*

Mark had been super-freaked when he found out it was the actual monkey he'd thrown away years ago. I asked him what he was going to do with it, and he said he didn't know. Probably throw it out again.

And yes: I *did* wonder if the new toy store had something to do with it. I didn't know how or why, but I just had an odd feeling there might be some connection between the monkey and Maxwell Kleagle's store.

I closed my eyes and tried to sleep, but I couldn't. I kept seeing Priscilla in the middle of the old hardware store, speaking my name. Oh, sure, she wasn't actually saying *my* name . . . but it sure was weird. And I kept seeing her in the alley as she appeared from the shadows, walking erratically and speaking.

Eric . . . Eric . . . Eric . . . .

And I kept reliving the whole episode at Mark's. Man! When he read the tag and found out the monkey was the same one he'd been given years ago, the same one he'd sold at the garage sale, he flipped his lid! I thought he was going to faint! He never thought he'd see that thing again in a million years . . . and yet, here it was. Somehow, it had mysteriously appeared on his doorstep.

How? Why?

I couldn't figure it out. But, I also knew I

couldn't stay awake all night and think about it. I *had* to get to sleep.

So, I tried counting sheep. I've always heard that if you're having a hard time falling asleep, it helps to count sheep. So, I pictured a large farm with hundreds of sheep. In my mind, I started counting. But, after I'd counted over three hundred sheep, I didn't feel any more tired than I had been when I started.

Then, in Madeline's bedroom across the hall, I heard Priscilla making noise. She'd malfunctioned again. It sounded like she was saying my name, over and over . . . just like she had done earlier in the day. After all: Mr. Kleagle had said her on/off switch was broken, and she would often turn on and off all by herself.

Suddenly, I was in the vicelike grip of dark horror. I snapped up in bed. My heart thundered as I suddenly remembered something.

It can't be! I thought. *I took Priscilla's batteries out before I gave the doll to Madeline!*

12

In my sister's room, I could still hear Priscilla repeating my name over and over. Yes, I knew Maxwell Kleagle had told me the doll wasn't saying *my* name, that her jaw was broken—but it still *sounded* like she was calling me!

And I don't think I would have been so frightened had I not removed the batteries. Sure, it was sort of eerie that a battery-powered doll would turn on and off by itself . . . but I had removed the batteries. *There was no way the doll should be doing anything!*

Then, Madeline started screaming. She, too, was scared by the doll that had seemingly come alive in her bedroom.

Chaos erupted. At the other end of the hall I could hear a commotion, and a faint light clicked on. Then, the bright hall light came on. I climbed out of bed just as Mom and Dad were rushing into Madeline's room. They turned her bedroom light on.

By now, Priscilla had stopped muttering. I could see the doll sitting in Madeline's chair, unmoving. She was facing Madeline's bed.

Mom and Dad were frantic. "What is it?" Dad asked. "What's wrong, Madeline?"

Madeline pointed to the doll. *"She's alive!"* she shrieked. *"She was talking and moving her legs!"*

Mom and Dad looked at the motionless doll in the chair.

"Honey, that's silly," Mom said. "You must've been dreaming."

"She was talking and moving her legs! She's alive!" Madeline said, continuing to point at the doll.

"Your doll isn't alive," Dad said. "It's only a doll."

"I heard her," I said, coming to my sister's defense. "She was talking. I could hear her from my bedroom. But, she shouldn't be, because I took the batteries out of her before I gave her to Madeline. Maxwell Kleagle said the doll is broken, and she sometimes turns on and off by herself."

"That solves it," Mom said. "I found the two red batteries on the coffee table. Madeline and I were trying to get her to work, but we couldn't, even with the batteries."

At that very moment, the doll came alive again, all on her own. It was so sudden and quick that even Mom and Dad jumped.

"Eric . . . Eric . . . Eric . . . ."

"She sounds like she's saying your name," Mom said as she picked up the doll. Priscilla was moving her legs back and forth, and her jaw was moving up and down.

"Eric . . . Eric . . . Eric . . . ."

"The on/off switch doesn't seem to shut her off," Mom said as she flipped the doll over in her hands. Then, she popped open the battery compartment. As soon as she removed the two batteries, Priscilla stopped.

"There," Mom said. "I've taken her batteries out. Now we can all get some sleep."

She returned the doll to Madeline's chair, but my sister shook her head. "No, no," she said.

"It's only a doll, Madeline," Dad insisted.

"I'm scared," my sister said, still shaking her head from side to side.

"How about we do this," Mom said. She picked up Priscilla, opened Madeline's closet door, and placed the doll inside, on the floor. Then, she closed the door. "All gone," she said. "Is that better?"

Madeline bobbed her head.

"Good," Dad said. "Now, go back to sleep." He bent over, pulled the covers up to Madeline's chin, and gave her a kiss on her cheek. "See you in the morning," he said.

I went back to my bedroom. Little by little, our house returned to normal. Mom clicked off Madeline's bedroom light, then my parents strode back down the hall to their room. The hall light clicked off, and the house was dark once again.

And finally, I was able to get to sleep. Oh, it took a few minutes, but I forced myself to stop thinking about talking dolls and monkeys that slapped cymbals together. Still, I had dreams of toys of all sorts, coming alive, chasing me. It was very frightening because no matter how fast I ran, the toys kept up with me, swirling around me, chasing me down. In my dreams, I couldn't get away from the toys that had taken on a life of their own.

When I woke up in the morning, I remembered my dreams and how frighteningly real they had seemed. Now that I was awake, I was no longer afraid.

Just dreams, I thought as I climbed out of bed.

But I was jolted by something I'd heard on television. Not long ago, I saw an old woman being interviewed on the news. She had won a lot of money in the lottery, and they asked her how she felt. She had said *'dreams do come true.'*

They had for her. She had dreamed of winning the lottery, and she had. Her dreams had come true.

Unfortunately, my dreams were going to come true, too . . . .

In the morning, I woke up later than usual. I hadn't fallen asleep until long after midnight, and I was still a little tired. Dad had already left for work, and Madeline was in her familiar place, sprawled out on her stomach in front of the television. Apparently, she wasn't too flipped out by what had happened the night before, because Priscilla was next to her. Like my sister, the doll was also on her stomach, but, since the doll couldn't move her head, her face was planted in the carpet.

I ate breakfast and got dressed. I hadn't planned on doing anything that day, and my mind bounced around different ideas.

I could go fishing with Mark and Shayleen again, I thought. *Or, we could go for a bike ride. If it got really hot, we could have a water balloon fight. Or, we could ride our skateboards. If it rained, we could go to the library.*

That's one of the great things about where we live. There's always something fun to do, any time of the year.

But, there was one thing I did *not* want to do . . . and that morning, I had to do it.

Wash the windows.

Oh, I didn't complain or anything. I knew that sooner or later, Mom would get around to asking me to do it. That morning, she did.

Reluctantly, I went to the kitchen and found the bottle of glass cleaner in the cupboard beneath the kitchen sink. Then, I grabbed the roll of paper towels from the counter. I figured I might as well start inside. When I'd finished indoors, I would go outside and make my way around the house.

I can't wait until my sister is old enough to do this, I thought. *Then, even if she doesn't have to do it on her own, at least she can help.*

It took me about an hour to clean the inside windows. I probably could have done them faster, but I wanted to make sure I got the corners clean. That's where all the dust and dirt can pile up, and if you don't keep them clean, the dirt will cake on the glass like cement. Then, it's almost impossible to get the grime off.

When I finished indoors, I went outside and started with the big window in the living room.

I didn't really mind cleaning the windows that morning. The sun was rising, and the sky was blue. The air was fresh and clean. Birds were chirping, and a few cars went by on the street. I saw a couple of people jogging. One of our neighbors, Mrs. Cooper, was pushing her baby in a carriage. She waved to me and joked that when I was done with the windows at our house, I could go to her home and clean her windows. I laughed, but then I thought it might be a way to make some money. Maybe people would pay me to clean their windows.

I had finished cleaning the windows on three sides of the house. The only ones left were in the backyard. The job would be finished in just a few minutes, and I'd be free the rest of the day.

Walking up to Madeline's bedroom window, I raised the bottle of window cleaner and was about to spray.

I stopped.

I dropped the water bottle, and it bounced to the grass at my feet.

The face of Priscilla stared back at me from the other side of the window!

I took a step backward.

Then another.

My eyes never left the horrifying vision unfolding before me. Priscilla glared at me from the other side of the glass! Her eyes were cold and menacing, and they seemed to be boring right into me.

And she was moving, too! Her head was slowly rising up, then down, up, then down.

Then, her head lowered . . . and vanished. Another face popped up.

My sister.

She had a silly grin on her face, and she was

giggling.

I should have known, I thought, heaving a sigh of relief. *It had only been Madeline, playing around.*

She opened the window. "Brazilla was just checking to see if you were doing a good job," she said.

I had to laugh. Madeline hadn't even tried to scare me. She was just playing with her new doll, having fun.

"Tell Priscilla I'm doing a great job," I said. "In fact, tell Priscilla that she can help, if she wants."

Madeline giggled. "Brazilla can't help wash windows!" she said. "She's just a dolly!" Then, she laughed, closed the window, and vanished.

I shook my head and smiled. My sister is pretty cute, and she can be funny sometimes.

When I finally finished the windows, I returned the bottle of glass cleaner to the cupboard beneath the sink. While I was placing the paper towels on the dispenser, Mom came into the kitchen.

"Thank you for doing that," she said.

"You're welcome," I replied.

"While you were outside, Mark called," Mom said. "He wants you to come over when you're finished with the windows."

"Did he say what he wanted?" I asked.

Mom shook her head. "He didn't. But he sounded worried. Maybe even a little scared."

Mark? I thought. *What would he be scared about? Did it have something to do with the monkey?*

And I had a gut feeling as I ran down the street, heading for his house. I don't know why or how, but I just *knew* it had something to do with that monkey he'd found on his porch.

And I was right.

I found both Mark and Shayleen sitting on Mark's porch. Shayleen was holding the monkey in her hands, inspecting it. Mark had a worried look on his face.

"What's wrong?" I asked.

He pointed to the monkey. "That thing kept turning on all night long," he said. "I never wound it up at all. But it would bang his cymbals a few times, then stop. I would fall asleep, and it would bang the cymbals again. It freaked me out!"

"What did you do?" I asked.

"I finally had to put him in the garage,"

Mark replied. "He kept waking me up. And Mom and Dad thought it was me, playing around. They got mad and wouldn't believe me when I told them the monkey was doing it all by himself."

Shayleen wound the key, and the monkey began frantically slapping the cymbals together. After a moment, it stopped.

"I have an idea," I said. "You might think I'm crazy . . . but what if this has something to do with the new toy store?"

"What would the toy store have to do with it?" Shayleen asked.

I shook my head. "I don't know," I said. "But I got a weird feeling yesterday when I was talking to the guy that's opening the store. I say we go back and talk to him."

"He's going to think we're crazy," Mark said.

"Maybe," I said with a shrug. "But so what? At least we'll have an answer, one way or the other. It can't hurt."

"All right," Mark said, "but *you* can do the talking. That way, he'll think *you're* the nutty one, not me."

"Fine with me," I said. "I talked to him

yesterday. He seemed like a nice guy, but I still got a weird feeling about the whole thing."

Mark stood up. Shayleen placed the monkey on the porch, then got to her feet. "You think he'll be at the toy store this morning?" she asked.

"Only one way to find out," I replied. "Let's go."

We started out across the lawn, but before we reached the sidewalk, we heard a noise from behind us.

We stopped walking, and froze.

A chill came over me. I looked at Shayleen, and she looked at me. Her eyes were wide, and her jaw hung open. Then, I glanced at Mark. His face was twisted in an expression of horror and shock.

Still, none of us had turned around to see what the noise was, because we all knew.

We *knew* where the noise was coming from, and what was causing it.

And when we finally *did* turn around, there was the monkey, sitting on the porch, banging his cymbals together . . . all by himself. He hadn't been wound up, but he was slapping the cymbals together.

"Come on," I whispered, and my voice trembled. *"Let's go to the toy store and see if we can figure out what's going on."*

16

We turned around and walked until the sounds of the monkey faded away, drowned out by the sounds of cars passing by and a few chirping birds.

"I can't understand how that thing could keep going off all night long," Mark said. "After all . . . he's a wind-up toy. If he's not wound-up, he's not supposed to work."

"I don't know, either," I replied. "But maybe Mr. Kleagle will know something."

We walked the rest of the way in silence, which was strange. Usually, when the three of us are together, we're always talking and chatting and laughing.

Not today.

A seriousness had come over the three of us. Not only did I wonder what was going on, I wondered if we were getting into something way over our heads. I found myself not wanting to go to the toy store.

What was I afraid of? Why?

Up ahead, I saw the old building come into view, and I could see the new sign in the window. The building looked the same as it had the day before, when I'd met Mr. Kleagle.

"He might not even be there," I said as we drew closer and closer.

"If he's not, we can always come back later," Shayleen said.

There was no sign of anyone around the old building. The ice cream store wasn't open yet, but *Lost Soles,* the secondhand shoe store was.

"Let's go through the alley to the back of the store," I suggested. "That's where Mr. Kleagle was yesterday. Maybe he's unloading things in the back."

We walked single file through the alley. There was a gray and white striped cat behind the garbage can. I didn't see him until he was by my foot, and when he ran off, I just about jumped out of my skin! I had surprised him, but I don't know who was scared more—the cat, or me!

"Silly thing," I said beneath my breath.

"We aren't going to get into trouble, are we?" Shayleen asked.

"No," I assured her. "I was here yesterday. Mr. Kleagle didn't seem to mind."

Well, maybe Mr. Kleagle didn't mind . . . but there was something that minded a great deal.

Something that, by the sounds of it, didn't want us there.

And we had no way of knowing it was lurking in the shadows, just a few steps away.

We all heard the noise at the same time. It came from within a stand of dense bushes behind the ice cream shop.

And there was no mistaking what it was: the growl of a dog.

An *angry* dog.

There was something odd about the noise he made, but, at the moment, I was too terrified to realize it.

We stopped walking. Although we couldn't see the dog, the growling and snarling sounded like it was close . . . only a few feet away.

I thought about running, but, often, if you

run from a dog, that just makes them chase you. So, I figured the best thing to do was to remain still. Maybe the dog would go away on his own, once he realized we weren't a threat.

"Where is he?" Shayleen whispered.

"I don't know," I said.

While the dog continued growling, I looked around. A large, white box truck was backed up to the rear doors of what soon would be the new toy store. There were large, colorful decorations on the side of the truck's box . . . paintings of various toys and games and such. Bold, bright letters spelled out: *Maxwell's House of Terrific Toys! World Famous!* We couldn't see inside the truck, but I was sure it was probably loaded with toys.

There was a ramp extending from the back of the truck to the rear door, and I figured the unloading had already begun. Which was exciting, of course . . . but right now, we had something else to worry about.

The bushes began to move. But when I saw the dog, I laughed.

It was only a little tiny poodle!

The growls he was making sounded like he

was a big, vicious animal, but the dog that emerged from the bushes was only ten inches tall!

"Hey, wait a minute," Mark said. "That's not a real dog at all. It's a toy!"

Mark was right! The dog's movements were jerky and stiff, similar to the way Priscilla, the doll, moved.

We laughed as the toy dog emerged from the bushes. He had curly, white fur and a blue collar, and he moved with stiff, robot-like motions. He sounded mean and menacing, but when we found out he was only a toy, it was funny. He'd really freaked us out!

"Scared by a toy dog," I said, and I reached down and picked it up. There was an on/off switch on the dog's belly . . . but I discovered the switch was already in the 'off' position.

"Another one that's not working right," I said. "I wonder how many defective toys Mr. Kleagle has?"

Mark pointed to the truck parked behind the toy store. "I don't know," he said, "but there's someone, right there. Is that him?"

Shayleen and I turned. Mr. Kleagle had

emerged from the back of the truck. He was wearing a yellow shirt with blue pants and red shoes. He hadn't spotted us yet.

"Yeah, that's him," I said.

"He sure dresses funny," Shayleen said.

We watched.

"Okay!" Mr. Kleagle said to someone in the truck. "Hop to it! Hup! Two, three, four! Hup! Two, three, four!"

Suddenly, a small toy soldier marched down the ramp, followed by another, and still another. We watched while over a dozen soldiers filed past Maxwell Kleagle.

"Jack-in-the-Boxes!" Maxwell said. "You're next!"

We watched in amazement as several Jack-in-the-Boxes slid down the ramp. They weren't walking, and no one was pushing or pulling them. They were moving all by themselves!

"That's impossible!" Shayleen hissed.

"Maybe they have little wheels or something," Mark whispered. *"Maybe they're rolling out."*

"I don't think so," I said quietly. *"I can hear the bottom of the boxes sliding on the ramp."*

The Jack-in-the-Boxes made their way down the ramp and vanished into the toy store.

"Dolls! You're next!" Mr. Kleagle bellowed. Soon, a line of dolls proceeded out of the truck, down the ramp, and into the toy store.

Now, all of this occurred while we were watching from the far side of the back of the building, where the alley opened up. We were so amazed and confused by what we were seeing, it never occurred to us that perhaps Mr. Kleagle didn't want anyone to see what was going on.

But when he turned and saw us, we could see the fire in his eyes and the anger on his face.

A hard lump formed in my throat. My skin crawled. A sheen of sweat glazed my forehead.

It was then we realized we were in the wrong place at the wrong time.

Maxwell Kleagle glared at us.

We stared back, unsure of what to do. As the dolls continued their march into the store, Mr. Kleagle started walking toward us.

Should we run? I wondered. *Were we going to get into trouble?*

"I don't think he's very happy with us," Mark whispered.

Mr. Kleagle's eyes never left us as he drew near. However, his expression changed as he got closer. I could see he had started to smile, and he didn't look anywhere near as mad as he had only moments before.

The lump in my throat softened, and I wiped the film of sweat from my forehead with the palm of my hand.

Maxwell Kleagle wagged his index finger as he approached us. But, he was smiling, too, so I didn't think we were in trouble.

"Curious children, aren't you?" he said.

"We didn't want to do anything wrong," I said. "We . . . we just wanted to see the store."

I was still holding the toy dog in my hand, and I held it out to Mr. Kleagle. "We found this toy dog in the bushes," I said. "I think his on/off switch isn't working."

Mr. Kleagle took the dog and frowned. "Thank you," he said. "I've been looking all over for this one."

I gestured to Mark and Shayleen. "These are my friends," I said. "This is Mark, and this is Shayleen."

Mr. Kleagle bowed politely. "It's nice to meet both of you," he said. "I'm afraid my store isn't ready to open quite yet."

"That's okay," I said. "Actually, we came because . . . well, Mark has a question."

"Hey!" Mark said sharply. He glared at me. "You said *you* would do the talking!"

Mr. Kleagle clasped his hands behind his back as he bent slightly forward, looking at Mark. "A question, is it?" he asked. "Go ahead, my boy. What is the burning question you must ask? Does it have to do with a certain . . . monkey?"

The three of us gasped.

He knew!

"Uh . . . y . . . yeah," Mark stuttered. He was nervous. "I got rid of that monkey a long time ago, and it showed up on my porch yesterday."

"Placed there by yours truly!" Mr. Kleagle said, clearly pleased with himself. "You see, I purchased that monkey at a flea market. That's where many of my toys come from. I collect fine toys from all over the world, from many different places. I purchased the monkey just a few days ago. When I saw the name on the tag, I thought that, perhaps, it belonged to someone. And maybe, just maybe, that someone wanted it back. I was easily able to find out where you lived. No one was at home when I arrived, so I left the toy on your front porch. Mystery solved!"

"Oh, okay," Mark said. He didn't tell Mr. Kleagle he'd sold the monkey at his garage sale a long time ago and really didn't want it back. After all . . . Mr. Kleagle had gone through the trouble of tracking Mark down. Mark wasn't going to tell him he no longer wanted the monkey.

"But the monkey bangs his cymbals together all by himself," I said. "Even when he's not wound up."

"All part of the magic of toys, wouldn't you say?" Mr. Kleagle replied. "After all . . . toys *should* have a little bit of magic, shouldn't they?" He glanced at Mark, then he looked at me.

"I guess so," I said, but I really wasn't sure what he meant. And he never explained further.

"When will the store be opening?" Shayleen asked.

"Oh, very soon, very soon," Maxwell Kleagle replied. His eyes twinkled. "Of course, I'm sure a few curious children would probably want to see just what's in store for them, would they not?"

"Oh, that would be great!" Shayleen replied. "I'd love to see!"

"Yeah!" Mark said. "We could tell all of our

friends and help you get the word out! We'll make sure everyone knows about your store!"

"Splendid!" Maxwell Kleagle said, clapping his hands several times. "I'll tell you what: you three come back tomorrow morning, and I will give you a personal, private tour of my store."

"I can't wait!" Shayleen said.

"Awesome!" said Mark.

"Yeah, that'll be cool," I said. But I wasn't as excited as Mark and Shayleen. Something wasn't adding up, and I didn't know what it was.

Very soon, however, I would realize we were already in trouble way over our heads . . . and it all began that night, after I went to bed.

Not much happened the rest of the day. It started to rain around lunchtime, so we spent a couple of hours in the afternoon playing cards at Shayleen's house. When I went home, I ate dinner. Mom made fried chicken, potatoes, and corn on the cob. Dad told us about his day at work, and he told us a bunch of really funny jokes.

But Madeline was acting strange. Not in a bad way, I guess. She was just being really quiet and not saying much. She didn't even laugh at Dad's jokes.

And she had Priscilla with her everywhere she went. If she went into her bedroom, she carried the doll with her. When she was watching television, Priscilla sat on her lap or next to her. She even took the doll into the bathroom with her when she took a bath before going to bed! And, of course, Priscilla was next to my sister as she fell asleep. The doll was propped on a pillow, eyes wide, as if she could actually *see*. I'm telling you—it was downright *eerie*.

"Your sister really loves that doll," Mom said as she poked her head in my bedroom to say good-night. "She's had it with her all day. She even put the batteries back in, to see if she can get the doll working right. It was very nice of that man to give it to her." Mom placed a glass of ice water on the night stand next to my bed, just like she does every night.

"Yeah," I said. "I'm glad she likes it."

Was that the truth, really?

No.

Really, I wasn't very glad at all. I had this strange feeling there was something really wrong with that doll, and I didn't know what it was. I'd read somewhere that feelings like that are called 'premonitions.' That's when you get a feeling or a suspicion about something in the future. For instance, if you think you might get a flat tire on your bike the next day . . . that would be a kind of premonition. Or, if you thought someone was going to get sick . . . that would be a premonition.

And, as Mom said good-night and turned the light off, as I pulled the covers up to my chin and stared out the window at the half-moon, I wondered if that's what I had about Madeline's new doll.

A premonition.

A warning of bad things to come.

And in a few short hours, my premonition wouldn't be a premonition anymore.

It would become reality.

20

Why is it that all of the really scary things seem to happen at night? Is it because it's dark and hard to see? Is it because there are noises at night that you never hear during the day? Our house makes noises once in a while: squeaks and groans, sighs and moans. But Dad said it's just the house settling. He said houses continue to settle for years and years.

Or, maybe scary things seem to happen more at night because shadows appear so menacing. There have been many times that shadows in my bedroom seemed to be in the shape of a monster or something. Once, I got scared by a shadow on my wall that looked like some sort of werewolf. I was sure I could actually see pointy ears, a snout, and long fangs. Actually, it was just a shadow created by some clothing draped over my chair. But my imagination got the best of me, and I could have sworn that I was seeing the shadow of a werewolf, right there in my bedroom.

Whatever the reasons, nighttime always seems to be the right time for getting scared out of your wits.

I fell asleep easily enough, but I woke up in the middle of the night. I had no idea what time it was, but I took a sip of water from the glass by my bed. The glass was cold and damp. I took a couple more sips, then returned it to the night stand.

I closed my eyes and thought about Maxwell Kleagle's toy store. Mark and Shayleen were really excited about getting a tour and seeing the inside of the store before anyone else.

I, on the other hand, was wary . . . and I couldn't figure out why. I guessed it was just a number of things together: the doll; the strange monkey that slapped his cymbals without being wound-up; and the way the toys emerged from the truck and went into the toy store on their own, when they were ordered to do so by Mr. Kleagle. I imagined at any other toy store, workers would have to haul the toys into the store in boxes, where they would unpack and unload them. Mr. Kleagle treated the toys like they were alive, like they could understand what he was saying. It was strange, to say the least.

But it would all be cleared up in the morning. I told myself I had no reason to worry, that it was all my imagination. There would be an explanation for everything, and after we toured the toy store, my suspicions would go away.

I was almost asleep when I heard a noise. At first, I thought it was Mom or Dad going into the kitchen. When they do this, I'll see their shadow pass by my open door.

But I didn't see a shadow, and when I heard the noise again, I sat up in bed. My sister's bedroom is directly across from mine, and her door was open. In her room, the only thing I could see was a shadowy portion of the foot of her bed. Other than that, I saw nothing. At the end of the hall, there is a night light in the bathroom. It's not very bright, but it gives off enough light so you can see where you're going, if you get up in the middle of the night.

I remained still for a moment, listening.

It was probably the house settling again, I thought. When I was little, I had often been very frightened by some of the normal sounds our house made at night. Dad says the house makes the same noises during the day, but because there are so many other noises and things going on, we rarely hear the subtle, quiet squeaks and creaks the house makes.

I was just about to lay back down when I heard the noise again. This time, it sounded like a squeaky floor board. There are several places in our house where the floor squeaks . . . but you have to step on them, of course.

In my sister's bedroom, something moved at the foot of her bed. My heart skipped a beat, and my imagination went wild.

It's the doll, I thought. *I know it is. I don't know how and I don't know why, but it's that doll. It's Priscilla.*

Sure enough, I could hear the doll making

that strange sound that made it seem like she was calling my name. It was very faint, however, like the doll was whispering.

"*Eric . . . Eric . . . Eric . . . .*"

My sister or my mom had probably put her batteries back in. I could hear the doll shuffling about, and then I saw her shadow.

Wait a second, I thought. *That shadow is too big to be Priscilla. In fact, that's not a doll at all. That's my sister!*

While I watched, my sister emerged from the dark shadows of her bedroom. In the dim light, she looked sleepy and dazed. Her movements were jerky and stiff, like she was having a hard time walking. She walked like—

Like Priscilla walked.

And she talked—

"*Eric . . . Eric . . . Eric . . . .*"

—the way Priscilla talked!

No! my mind screamed. *This can't be happening! Somehow, the doll has taken over my sister!*

21

Madeline repeated my name louder and louder, until she was nearly shouting.

"*Eric . . . Eric . . . Eric . . . ERIC!*"

Talk about being freaked out! I've never been frightened by my little sister, but, then again: what I was seeing wasn't Madeline at all!

Her shouting woke my parents. The hall light clicked on, and Madeline stopped speaking.

"What's wrong?" I heard Mom say. Then, I saw her and Dad in the hall, kneeling down around my sister.

Madeline looked dazed and confused. "Where . . . where am I?" she asked.

"You're home, in the hallway," Mom replied. "You don't remember how you got here?"

Madeline shook her head. "No," she peeped.

"You must've been sleepwalking," Dad said. "You were calling for your brother, it sounded like."

"She was," I said, and Mom and Dad turned to look at me. "I heard her," I continued. "She was walking really weird and calling my name. It freaked me out!"

"I want to go to bed," Madeline sniffed. I thought she was going to cry, but she didn't. She balled her fists and rubbed her eyes.

Mom took my sister by the hand and led her back to her room. Madeline climbed into bed, and Mom tucked her in.

My dad's silhouette darkened my bedroom door. "How long was she in the hall?" he asked.

"Not long," I replied.

"We'll all have to keep an eye on her if she's sleepwalking," Dad said. "Can you do that?"

"Yeah," I said as I lay back on my pillow. Then I thought: *That's silly. How can we keep an eye on her if we're all sleeping?*

I also kept wondering: *Was Madeline really sleepwalking?* Her movements—even the way she spoke my name—were identical to Priscilla's. I know it sounds crazy, and that's what I told myself. I told myself there was no way a doll could take over a human being. Maybe in a book or a movie, but not in real life.

Things like that just can't happen.

Then again, I knew very little about Maxwell Kleagle and his toy store.

Within hours, however, I would know *everything*. Within hours, Mark, Shayleen, and I would know the horrible truth about Maxwell Kleagle and his terrifying toys.

22

In the morning, Mom, Dad, Madeline, and I were seated at the table, eating scrambled eggs, bacon, and toast.

"Do you remember walking in your sleep?" Mom asked Madeline as she poured a glass of orange juice.

Madeline shook her head from side to side while chewing a piece of toast.

"Nothing at all?" Mom asked.

Madeline swallowed. "Nope," she said.

"You were sleepwalking and calling out your brother's name," Dad said. "You don't remember it?"

Madeline bit into a piece of bacon and shook her head again. For whatever reason, she had no knowledge of what had happened in the hallway the night before.

Mom and Dad didn't ask her anything more about her sleepwalking episode. We finished breakfast, and I helped Mom wash and dry the dishes. Madeline went to her bedroom, retrieved Priscilla, and carried her into the living room to watch television.

"So, what are your plans today?" Mom asked as I looped the dish towel around the handle on the refrigerator door.

"Oh, not much," I said. "Mark and Shayleen and I are going to the new toy store. The owner said he'd give us a tour, even though he's not open yet."

"That'll be fun," Mom said.

"I hope so," I said.

After I changed out of my pajamas and into a pair of shorts and a T-shirt, I walked over to Mark's house. The sky was gray, and it looked like it might rain. It was hot, too . . . but there was nothing unusual about that.

But something weird happened at Mark's house.

When I knocked on the Bruder's front door, Mark's mom answered it.

"Hi, Mrs. Bruder," I said.

"Hello, Eric," she said.

"Is Mark home?"

Mrs. Bruder nodded. "Yes, he is," she replied. "He's in his room."

Then she frowned, and a look of concern came over her face.

"Is something wrong?" I asked.

"I don't *think* so," Mrs. Bruder said. "It's just that, well, last night, he did something strange."

"What?" I asked. A lump began to grow in my throat, and my heart beat faster.

"In the middle of the night, his father and I were awakened by a noise in Mark's room. When we went to see if something was wrong, we found Mark on the floor with that silly monkey. The monkey was slapping its cymbals together. Its eyes were flashing. And Mark seemed to be doing the same thing: slapping his hands together in front of him. It was like he was imitating the monkey."

117.

Or the monkey was making him do it, I thought, as I recalled the bizarre incident with Madeline the night before.

"I asked him about it this morning," Mrs. Bruder continued, "but he didn't remember doing it. Have you noticed him acting strange lately?"

I shook my head. "No," I replied. "I haven't noticed anything."

"I'm sure it was nothing," Mrs. Bruder said. "It's just that he's never done anything like that before."

"What did you do?" I asked.

"When we woke him up," Mrs. Bruder said, "he was confused. He couldn't remember how he came to be sitting on the floor. He climbed back into bed and fell asleep. I took the monkey and put it on his bookshelf."

Just then, Mark walked into the living room and saw me standing on the porch.

"There you are," Mrs. Bruder said to him. "Eric is here." She strode off, and Mark walked to the door.

"How's it going?" I asked.

"Good," Mark replied. "Have you seen

Shayleen?"

"No," I said. "But I'm sure she'll be here soon."

Mark walked outside and closed the door behind him. "I can't believe we're going to get a tour of the toy store before it's open!" he said.

I was going to ask him about what his mom had told me, about how she had found him in his room, imitating the monkey, but I decided not to. After all, his mom said he didn't remember the incident.

Just like my little sister, I thought. *She didn't remember sleepwalking.*

Something weird was going on, that was for sure.

But, if I thought what had happened to Madeline and Mark was weird, it was nothing compared to what we were about to experience in Maxwell Kleagle's toy store.

23

It wasn't long before Shayleen showed up, and the three of us were on our way to the toy store. Cars and trucks ambled along the street, their drivers and passengers on their way to work. The sky was still cloudy and gray. It hadn't started to rain yet, but the air felt heavy and damp.

We approached the toy store and stopped on the sidewalk in front, staring in disbelief. Some big changes had occurred overnight. First of all, the small window sign was gone. It had been replaced with an even bigger sign that covered the entire window. In fact, both windows were covered with gigantic signs that read:

Maxwell's House of Terrific Toys! The finest, most wonderful toys in the entire world! Strange and magical toys and games! You name it, Maxwell's got it! OPENING THIS WEEKEND!

And the store had been painted! Before, it had been a dirty brown, and large spots of paint had chipped away from the brick like it had been gnawed by a giant rodent. Now, the store was bright white, covered with polka dots of all colors and sizes. It sure looked a lot different than it had the day before!

"Hey, the store will be open in a couple of days!" Mark exclaimed.

"I can't believe the entire store was painted in one day," I said, marveling at the art work.

"Yeah, but it looks cool," Shayleen said.

It was still early, and the ice cream and secondhand shoe stores were still closed. There was no sign of anyone around . . . until the front door of the store opened. The door opened . . . but there was no one there.

It's like a mouth, I thought as the door slowly swung open wide. *It's like a hungry mouth, waiting for food. Beyond that door is a wagging tongue and long, sharp fangs, ready to devour all who enter.*

"Where is Mr. Kleagle?" Mark asked. "Did he open the door?"

I shrugged. "I don't know," I said. "I don't see him. It's as if the door opened all by itself."

I wasn't sure I wanted a tour of the toy store, after all. Too many strange things had been happening, both with Priscilla the doll and Mark's monkey. I couldn't figure it out, but there was something really wrong with the toys—and the mysterious Maxwell Kleagle.

"Let's go have a look," Shayleen said, and the three of us started walking to the front door. Mark reached it first, and he cautiously peered inside.

"Whoah!" he exclaimed. *"You guys aren't going to believe this!"*

24

Shayleen and I huddled up behind Mark, who was leaning in the doorway. The three of us knotted together and looked cautiously inside.

Everything had changed—and I mean *everything*. The inside of the old building looked brand new. It had a fresh coat of paint we could still smell. The walls had all sorts of colorful things painted on them: animals, fish, and toys of all sorts. Racks and shelves had been set up along the walls, and even more racks created aisles on the floor. Toys of every imaginable shape and size filled the entire room. It was unbelievable! I'd never seen any toy store like it before in my life.

"How could this have been done in just one day?" Shayleen asked. "The place has been painted, inside and out. Even the floor shines like new."

"Mr. Kleagle must have had a lot of people helping him," Mark said.

"Nobody could have done this in one day," I said, shaking my head. "Not even if they worked through the night."

The three of us stood in the doorway, looking at everything. There were so many different toys of all shapes and sizes. Tiny dolls, no bigger than my hand, sat on shelves. Some dolls were nearly as big as I was, and they stood against the far wall. Model airplanes and rockets hung from the ceiling. Colorful stuffed animals were piled on the floor in a corner. A 50-gallon drum was filled with plastic balls of all sizes and colors.

And somewhere, music began to play. It was very faint at first, but it grew louder as we listened.

"What's that?" Shayleen whispered.

We listened to the faint, glass-like sounds, but we couldn't tell from which direction the music was coming.

"It sounds like a music box," I said.

The sound leveled off and continued. We listened, but we still couldn't pinpoint the location of the music. It seemed to be all around us: the floors, the walls, even the ceiling. It was strange, but it was also calm and soothing at the same time.

"Mr. Kleagle?" I called out.

There was no answer.

"Anybody home?" Mark said.

Still, there was no answer. The hidden music box played on, and the toys stared back at us, silent and still, watching.

They are *watching us,* I thought. *Every single toy in here seems to be watching us, waiting. Waiting for us to come inside.*

Suddenly, I didn't want to be at the toy store any longer. I was overcome with such a strong sense of doom and danger that I felt like turning and running away. I would run and run and never look back, and I would never return to the store.

Eric, you're just being silly, I told myself.

You're freaked out about some goofy toys. There's nothing to worry about.

And besides: I had two friends with me. We were together, and we'd look out for each other. Nothing could go wrong.

"Let's go inside and have a look around," Mark said. "Mr. Kleagle has to be around here, somewhere."

He took a step through the door.

Shayleen followed.

The strange music box played on.

Toys watched.

I followed Shayleen, unaware that the three of us had not only stepped into the toy store . . . we'd stepped into a nightmare.

25

As soon as we entered the store, things began to change. First, our surroundings dimmed. We hadn't noticed any lights on, but after we'd walked through the door, the light seemed to fade, as if the sun was going down. It was really strange. The music changed, too. It had seemed so light and airy and happy, and now it had become sinister and dark.

And the *toys*.

At first, they all looked happy and fun. Now, however, they appeared threatening and angry. The dolls seemed to be silently hissing at us, and their eyes seemed to watch our every move.

"Mr. Kleagle?" I called out. "We're . . . we're here for the tour. But if this isn't a good time, we can come back."

We waited.

Our surroundings grew darker still, and the only light came from the open doorway behind us. The dark music droned on, like the theme from some bizarre dream.

"I don't know if we should be here," Shayleen said. "This place is giving me a bad case of the creeps."

"Mr. Kleagle?" I called out again.

Still no answer.

In front of us, there was a sudden, loud, snapping sound. We jumped as a Jack-in-the-Box popped up, its head and arms bobbing and weaving back and forth. He was colorful and looked like a court jester, with tiny gold bells at the corners of his star-shaped, green hat.

"Man, that thing scared me for a second!" Mark exclaimed.

And that's when the toy began to speak.

"Howdy!" the Jack-in-the-Box said. "What's your name?"

At first, we were too stunned to speak. Then, Mark laughed. "Hey," he said, "that's kind of cool!"

"Howdy!" the Jack-in-the-Box repeated. "What's your name?"

Might as well play along, I thought. "I'm Eric," I said. "This is Mark and Shayleen."

"Eric, Mark, and Shayleen," the toy said to our amazement.

"Hey!" Shayleen said. "It learned our names! It must have some sort of computer chip or something!"

"Computer chip?" the toy said. The box began sliding toward us. "Computer chip? I don't have a computer chip. None of us have computer chips."

The toy continued to slide toward us, and the three of us took a step back.

"But . . . but you're just a toy," Mark stammered. Fear was heavy in his voice.

"Come on," I whispered. *"Let's get out of here."*

The toy stopped in the middle of the floor and began laughing. It was an awful, cackling laugh that seemed to grind in my ears.

"Get out of here?!?!" the Jack-in-the-Box taunted. *"Get out of here?!?! You won't be going anywhere for a long, long, time!"*

I'd had enough, and so had Mark and Shayleen. Whatever was going on in the toy store, whatever these toys were, we didn't want anything to do with them.

"Come on!" I shouted. The three of us spun . . . and that's when the door slammed shut, all by itself!

26

We were in a lot of trouble, and we knew it.

For a moment, I thought I was dreaming. Everything was too unbelievable, too unreal to be happening. Toys don't talk; they're not alive. They can't communicate. And doors don't close all by themselves.

I tried pushing the door open, but it wouldn't budge. Shayleen and Mark helped push, too, but it was no use. We were locked inside.

Behind us, the Jack-in-the-Box slid closer. "Don't you just hate it when that happens?" he said. Then, he let out another round of horrific, cackling laughter.

We turned to face the terrifying toy, only to find more toys around the store coming to life. They were slowly moving about, as if they were waking from a deep sleep. Dolls seemed to stretch, moving their arms and legs, and so did the stuffed animals.

And they were all looking at us.

"The back door!" I shouted, and the three of us sprang, leaping over the Jack-in-the-Box and bolting for the other side of the store. All the while, the same, dirge-like, haunting music played on. It was if we were in some sort of Halloween haunted house, only this was for *real*.

The back door was locked. We pushed and pulled, but it wouldn't budge an inch.

We turned around.

The toy store was chaotic. All around us, toys were coming to life. Dolls were chatting, laughing, but we couldn't understand what they were saying. A monkey was doing somersaults on the floor. Jack-in-the-Boxes were sliding along under their own power, their heads and arms bobbing from side to side. Toy soldiers marched. It was complete and total madness, to say the least.

Suddenly, one of the stuffed animals—a lion—leapt into the air, lunging for us, roaring just like a real lion! He landed on the floor near our feet.

Afraid that he might attack us, I did the only think I could do: I struck out with my right foot, kicking the stuffed animal back to the other side of the room. The lion flew threw the air, tumbling round and round until he hit the far wall and fell to the floor.

Other stuffed animals began leaping at us, and many toys began moving in our direction. The dolls were particularly creepy with their arms outstretched and their stone-cold eyes. They looked like girl-zombies, parading toward us.

So far, we had succeeded in keeping the stuffed animals and other toys away from us. Sooner or later, however, we would be overwhelmed. There were just too many of them. I didn't know what they wanted or what they were capable of doing, and I didn't want to hang around to find out!

"Over there!" Shayleen shouted, pointing.

"There's another door!"

We hadn't noticed it before, because the door was painted to look just like the wall. We had no idea where it led to or if it was locked—but we had to try. Maybe it led outside.

We ran to it, all the while kicking toys out of our way. It seemed like all of them were after us and were attacking in full force, like an organized army.

The door is going to be locked, I know it, I thought dismally, but was surprised to find the doorknob turning in my hand.

The door opened!

I pulled it back, and we saw wooden steps descending into darkness. There was a light switch on the wall, and when I flicked it up, a light at the bottom of the stairs bloomed.

"It's a basement!" I said. *"Go!"*

Shayleen and Mark raced past me. They took the wooden steps two at a time, and their footsteps echoed loudly. I pulled the door shut—and just in time, too. Several toy soldiers were close to reaching us, and if I hadn't shut the door at that moment, I'm not sure what would have happened.

More good luck: the door had a bolt lock, and I wasted no time securing it. It made a loud clunk as it slammed into place.

I could hear the sounds of the toys on the other side of the door, banging and pounding. Again, I had that fleeting feeling that I was dreaming, that I would suddenly wake up and find myself in my own bed, in my bedroom.

But that didn't happen. What was going on around us was real, all right. It was just as real as Mark or Shayleen or me. I didn't know how or why, and, at the moment, I didn't care. All I wanted to do was get out of the horrible toy store alive.

Mark and Shayleen reached the bottom of the stairs. I could still hear pounding from the door at the top of the stairs. The toys, apparently, weren't going to give up easily.

Suddenly, at the bottom of the stairs, Mark and Shayleen gasped. I raced down the steps, stopped, and turned to see what they were looking at. I had expected to see more toys or something of that sort.

Wrong.

It was an alien space creature!

27

We stared in shock and disbelief at the strange, silver creature on the far side of the empty basement. He was sitting on the floor, leaning back against the wall. He was human-shaped, but he was all silver and gray. I could see two black slits where his eyes were, and another slit where his nose poked out.

Wait a minute, I thought. *That's not a space alien . . . that's a human! But why does he look so strange, like he's wearing a costume?*

The creature—or whatever it was—tried to move, but couldn't.

"What *is* that thing?" Shayleen asked.

"It's an alien from another planet!" Mark exclaimed.

"I don't think it is," I said, and I walked across the cement floor. The alien made some grunting and groaning sounds and tried to move.

Very quickly, I knew we weren't looking at a space alien . . . but a real, live human being—*wrapped in silver duct tape!*

"Mark! Shayleen!" I called out. *"Come help me!"*

Mark and Shayleen raced to my side as I bent over the taped human. I wasn't sure who it was, but I had a good idea it would turn out to be Maxwell Kleagle.

And I was right!

As we unwound the sticky tape from his body, I recognized his clothing. But when we got to his head, we couldn't take the tape off!

"Ouch! Ouch! Ouch!" Mr. Kleagle said. "You're pulling my hair out!"

The tape was too sticky! We were able to get the tape away from his face, though, and as soon as his mouth was unbound, he started to speak.

"Those infernal toys!" he said. "They did this to me!"

"Are you all right?" Shayleen asked.

Mr. Kleagle stood. He looked a little silly with all that silver tape still on his head. But he didn't look like he was hurt.

"I'm fine," he said. "Thank you, all of you. But now we must do something about the toys."

We could still hear the faint pounding and banging coming from the door at the top of the stairs on the other side of the basement. In my mind, I could see an army of colorful toys, all trying to break the door down.

"What's going on here?" Mark asked. "What's up with those toys coming to life?"

Maxwell Kleagle sat down on the floor and put his head in his hands. Thick strings of silver tape fell over his shoulders. "It's all my fault, I'm afraid. I didn't mean for this to happen. They just . . . they just got out of hand, that's all. I didn't think it would go this far."

"*What* would go this far?" I asked.

"This whole thing," Mr. Kleagle said. "I just wanted children to have fun and unique toys they

141

couldn't get anywhere else. But my plan backfired. My toys have become . . . *monsters.*"

"Maybe you should start at the beginning," Shayleen said.

So, that's what Maxwell Kleagle did: he told us everything. He told us about the toys, what had happened to them, and what they were attempting to do.

And it didn't take us long to realize that we might not make it out of the basement.

Not alive, anyway.

"Everything started a few years ago, with an experimental battery I invented," Maxwell Kleagle explained. "I wanted to create a battery that would last longer than any other battery in the world. I hoped it would make my toys last and last, and it would make me—and my toys—famous.

"But something amazing happened!" Mr. Kleagle's eyes widened as he continued explaining. "The batteries not only lasted a long time, they somehow made the toys come to life. The energy in the battery seemed to give the toys minds of their own."

"That's what happened to Priscilla!" I said.

"Yes, that is correct," Mr. Kleagle said with a nod. "The longer the batteries were in the toys, the stronger each toy became. Children have loved the toys, because they seem so much more real. It's like they have a new friend, and not just a toy. Of course, not all of the toys I have require batteries. Those toys are of no danger to anyone, of course."

"But the toys upstairs attacked us!" Mark said.

Mr. Kleagle nodded. "Me, too, I'm afraid. They've become too powerful. Up until today, they would listen to my commands. In fact, the toys painted the store last night. I commanded them to do it, and they did, in the middle of the night, when no one could see them. It was quite a sight, indeed! They worked together and completed painting the inside and outside of the building before sunrise. Today, however, they will no longer obey my commands."

"Is that how you got wrapped up in duct tape?" Shayleen asked.

Again, Mr. Kleagle nodded. "Yes, yes," he said. "It was the work of the toy soldiers and the dolls. I couldn't stop them. They have become very clever. They have their own plans for this toy store. I never thought they would turn on me. Not in a million years."

"They waited until we were inside the toy store before they locked us in," I said. "That's when they attacked us."

"They've got to be stopped," Maxwell Kleagle said. "In fact, the longer someone is around the toy, it becomes possible for the toy to hypnotize the human. Then, the toy can order the person to do whatever they want. They must be stopped, before they cause much more trouble for people in the city."

"But what about my monkey?" Mark asked. "He's just a wind-up toy."

"Not true," Mr. Kleagle said. "The key in his back operates his arms only. He has a single battery to power his blinking eyes. The compartment is located in his leg. I know, because I put in one of my experimental batteries before I took him to your house."

"I never knew that," Mark said. "But I guess it makes sense."

"As if *any* of this can make sense," Shayleen added.

"You must believe me," Mr. Kleagle said. "I had no idea that this would happen. I knew the toys seemed to be getting smarter, but I never knew they would do something like this. Like I said: we must stop these toys."

"But how?" Shayleen asked. "There are so many of them."

"I can't do it alone," Mr. Kleagle said. "They'll just overpower me again. In fact, after they bound me with duct tape, I thought I'd never get free. You children came along at just the right time."

"Not the right time for us," I said glumly.

"But you found me and were able to free me," Mr. Kleagle said. "Alone, I don't think I can stop the toys. They've gained too much power. But together, the four of us might have a chance."

The banging coming from the basement door grew louder. Several crashes were heard from upstairs.

"You see?" Mr. Kleagle said. "They're getting smarter, even as we speak. But we might be able

146

to stop them."

As we listened, Mr. Kleagle explained his plan. And, as much as I didn't want to go along with it, I quickly realized it was the only chance we had. We were trapped, and the toys were going to force us to fight. One of two groups would survive the battle: us or the toys.

Who would win?

"We'll get each toy one at a time," Mr. Kleagle explained. "It's going to be tricky. We'll need to open the basement door just enough to let in one or two toys at a time. Then, we'll close the door, capture the toys, and remove the batteries."

"But you said the toys are getting stronger and stronger," Mark said.

"Not necessarily stronger," Mr. Kleagle said, "but *smarter*. They use the energy in the batteries as kind of an artificial intelligence."

"What's 'artificial intelligence?'" Shayleen asked.

"It means they seem to have an ability to

think on their own, but they really can't. Any intelligence they have is coming from the energy in the batteries."

"Oh," Shayleen said. "I get it. If we take the batteries out of the toys, they lose their ability to think."

"Exactly," Mr. Kleagle said. "And that's what we must do. One by one, toy by toy. Alone, I can't do it. But together, we can . . . I think."

His plan was for the four of us to remain at the top of the stairs, by the door. He would open the door and allow one or two toys to get in. The three of us would grab the toy and remove the batteries. It would take us a while, but Mr. Kleagle was confident we would be able to get all of the toys, if we could keep them from ganging up on us.

"The sooner, the better," I said. "Let's get started. This might take a while."

Mr. Kleagle got to his feet, and the four of us strode across the basement floor and climbed the steps. Mr. Kleagle looked sillier than ever, with his bright clothing and a long mane of silver duct tape cascading down his back.

The sounds coming from the other side of the basement door were louder than ever. It sounded like the door would come crashing down at any moment. We could even see the door vibrate and shake when a toy hit it.

And I will admit: I was more than just a little scared. Now that we knew the toys really *were* dangerous, that they had the capacity to think on their own, I was worried. We were going to have to act fast and be careful.

"Ready?" Mr. Kleagle asked. He had one hand on the door handle and one hand on the bolt lock.

"Just be careful," Mark said.

"I'll try to let one or two in at a time," Mr. Kleagle said. "Here we go."

He slid the deadbolt back, turned the handle, and opened the door just a tiny bit.

Immediately, several toys tried to squeeze through the thin opening. I saw the furry hands of some stuffed animal groping at the door. A single doll hand waggled, trying to pry the door open farther.

"Grab a toy and pull it through!" Mr. Kleagle

ordered.

I grabbed one of the stuffed animal's paws and pulled. The door opened a tiny bit more, and a yellow and black stuffed tiger slipped through. *I was actually holding a tiger!*

Not a real tiger, of course. It was only a stuffed animal, about the size of a house cat . . . but the way the thing struggled in my hands, he sure felt like he was alive!

And he was trying to bite me! Although his teeth were only plastic, I knew the thing could really hurt me if he was able to sink them into my skin.

"His batteries are in his belly!" Mr. Kleagle shouted. He had thrown his body against the door to keep the toys from forcing it open even more than it was.

It was a struggle. The tiger kept squirming around in my hands, trying to get away. Several times, he snarled and tried to bite me, but I finally managed to pop open the battery compartment in his belly. Two batteries spilled out and bounced down the stairs. Instantly, the stuffed animal went limp.

"I did it!" I exclaimed.

"We still have a lot more to go!" Mr. Kleagle said. *"Let's keep at it!"*

We worked together. Mr. Kleagle opened the door a tiny bit, while Mark, Shayleen, and I took turns grabbing a toy and pulling it through the small opening. The trick was to make sure the door didn't open very far, because all of the toys were trying to get through at once.

One by one, we grabbed toys, found their battery compartments, and removed the batteries. Once this was done, we tossed the toys down the stairs. Soon, there was a growing pile of toys at the bottom of the steps.

But there were still many more toys to go, and Mr. Kleagle was having a hard time holding the door. The toys were relentless in their attack, and I knew if they all got through at once, we'd be in for a lot of trouble. We'd managed to hold our own for the time being . . . until suddenly, the door was flung violently open, knocking the four of us off balance and sending us tumbling down the basement stairs!

The tumble down the stairs was painful, but none of us were injured seriously. We all received a few minor scrapes and bruises; that was it. Thankfully, the large pile of toys at the bottom of the steps provided a soft landing. Otherwise, the four of us would have smacked into hard cement. That would have hurt!

We quickly got to our feet and looked up. At the top of the stairs, several large dolls stood, along with a Jack-in-the-Box and a small army of toy soldiers. The soldiers only stood a foot tall, but they looked like they meant *business*. And the dolls looked nasty, too. It was hard to believe such an innocent toy could look so menacing. Even the Jack-in-the-Box looked sinister and mean.

"We're in big trouble, now," Mark said.

And he was right. Suddenly, toys began flooding down the stairs. Some of them, like the Jack-in-the-Box, tumbled and bounced end over end. It was like an avalanche of toys rolling down upon us.

"Get them!" Mr. Kleagle ordered. *"Quickly!"*

We scrambled like crazy, snapping up toys, locating their battery compartments, and taking the batteries out. It was chaos and madness! Toys were banging into me. Several large dolls wrapped their arms around my legs and tried to pull me to the floor. A stuffed monkey bit my ankle, but I kicked him away.

Mr. Kleagle tried unsuccessfully to climb the stairs to close the door. Too many toys came at him, knocking him off balance. Once, he nearly fell, and finally had to retreat to the bottom of the stairs.

"Look out!" Shayleen suddenly cried, as a model airplane soared overhead, buzzing like an angry bee. Mr. Kleagle, however, was ready. He

grabbed a stuffed animal and flung it at the tiny plane, knocking it out of the air. It crashed to the ground and snapped in dozens of plastic pieces.

More toys came down the steps. Many of them couldn't walk down, but that didn't matter. Even if they fell and tumbled, they quickly regained control of themselves when they hit the floor.

Still, we tried to grab as many as we could. They kept coming at us, wave after wave. Some of them—particularly the stuffed animals—were really strong. A stuffed green snake, nearly five feet long, wrapped itself around Shayleen and began to constrict.

"He's squeezing me!" she shouted. Quickly, I found the snake's battery compartment and removed the two batteries. The snake went limp and fell to the floor like a giant, fuzzy noodle.

The pile of toys around us grew. Batteries were scattered all over the floor. But there were fewer toys attacking.

"It's working!" Mr. Kleagle exclaimed as he grabbed a soldier and picked it up. The toy struggled and kicked, but Mr. Kleagle quickly

removed the batteries from a small compartment in the toy's back.

Finally, the onslaught of toys ceased. No more came through the open basement door and down the stairs. The four of us stood silently for a moment, waiting for more toys to attack. None did.

"It worked," Mark said with a heavy sigh. We were all out of breath from working so hard and moving around so much.

I looked around. Toys were piled on top of each other, scattered all around our feet. It looked like there had been an explosion or something!

"Yes, we succeeded!" Mr. Kleagle said. "And I won't be using my experimental batteries anymore, that's for sure. People aren't going to buy my toys if they know they're going to be attacked."

A horrible thought suddenly came to my mind. My skin went cold and broke out in gooseflesh.

"Priscilla!" I exclaimed. *"My sister put her batteries back in! She was trying to get the doll to work!"*

Mark's eyes bulged. *"And my monkey! He's at my house . . . and my mom is home!"*

"You must hurry!" Mr. Kleagle ordered. "The toys are too powerful! You've got to stop them! I'll stay here to make sure we've taken care of the toys in the store!"

"I'll stay here and help Mr. Kleagle!" Shayleen said.

Mark and I raced up the steps. We burst through the open doorway and looked around.

The toy store was in shambles. Toys that weren't battery-operated lay all around. Plastic balls of all different sizes and colors were strewn everywhere. A shelf had been knocked over. One of the overhead lights had been broken, and there were pieces of glass all over the floor. Mr. Kleagle had a huge mess to clean up, that was for sure.

I would've stayed and helped, but I was too worried about my mom and my sister. They were home alone with Priscilla, and I had to get there in time to stop her.

Of course, as I raced out of the toy store and sprang down the sidewalk, I had no way of knowing it was already too late. I had no way of knowing that, ever since I had left, Priscilla had gone to work on both Mom and Madeline.

And when I got to the house, Priscilla was ready and waiting . . . .

31

The first thing I saw when I threw open the front door was the doll.

Priscilla.

She was standing in the middle of the living room as if she had been waiting for me to return.

What was even *more* horrifying: Mom and Madeline were seated on the couch, looking dazed. Their eyes were glossy, staring off into space. It looked like they were in a trance of some sort.

Priscilla began to speak. Her words were jumbled and awkward, but I could understand her all too clearly.

"So . . . good of . . . you . . . to come," she said with a wicked grin. "We've . . . we've been wait . . . waiting for . . . for you."

Mom and Madeline repeated what the doll said. They spoke like robots.

"Waiting for you," they said, and their voices were unnatural and without emotion.

Priscilla has hypnotized them! I thought with growing horror. *It's already started! She's taking over Mom and Madeline! I have to stop her before she hypnotizes me!*

Without warning, the doll rushed toward me. I was amazed at how fast and strong she was! In seconds, she had not only wrapped her plastic arms around my leg, but she was able to knock me backward. I fell, barely missing the coffee table.

"Waiting for you," Mom and Madeline repeated in their robot-like voices. *"Waiting for you . . . ."*

Priscilla gripped my legs so hard that it hurt. *"Mom!"* I screamed. *"Madeline! Help me!"*

It was no use. They were under Priscilla's spell and paid no attention to me. *"Waiting for you,"* they repeated, over and over.

I grabbed Priscilla by the hair just in time, as she had reared her head back and opened her mouth. I knew she was going to try to bite me.

Suddenly, I began to feel dizzy. I could hear a voice in my mind, gnawing at my brain. It wasn't my voice, and it wasn't the voice of Mom or Madeline.

It's Priscilla! She's trying to hypnotize me! She's using her energy to get inside my mind! She's trying to take control of me . . . just like she's done with Mom and Madeline!

I focused hard and tried to push her out of my thoughts. She was still gripping my leg, holding it with both hands. I had her by the hair with one hand. With the other, I grabbed at her back until I found the battery compartment. I slapped at it and the cover snapped open.

Just then, Priscilla rolled to the side. She never let go of my leg, and she forced me to roll with her. I couldn't believe how strong the doll was!

On the couch, Mom and Madeline sat, still staring off into space, repeating what Priscilla had said.

"Waiting for you . . . ."

I had only one chance, and I knew it. With a sudden burst of energy, I raised my leg and Priscilla into the air and slammed the doll as hard as I could onto the living room floor.

Her grip lessened.

She stopped moving.

I saw two red batteries tumble onto the carpet, and I rolled to the side. Priscilla remained where she was, face down on the floor.

Mom and Madeline suddenly came out of their trance. It was weird: they snapped right out of it and had no recollection of what had just happened!

"Oh, hello, Eric," Mom said. "I didn't see you come in."

"You . . . you didn't?" I asked.

"No," Mom said. "But I'm glad you're home. The lawn needs to be mowed."

Madeline looked at her doll on the floor. Then, she glared at me. "What did you do to Brazilla?!?!" she demanded.

They had no idea what had just happened! They had no idea I had probably just saved their lives!

"I didn't do anything to your doll," I assured her. I scooped up the two batteries and stuffed them into my pocket. Then, I stood. I picked up Priscilla and handed her to Madeline. "See?" I said. "She's fine. Nothing wrong with her at all. Not anymore, anyway."

Madeline hugged Priscilla, bounded from the couch, and walked to her room.

"Mom," I said urgently, "do you mind if I go to Mark's house? I won't be gone long, and I promise I'll mow the lawn as soon as I get home."

"That's fine," Mom said. "Just don't be gone long."

"I won't," I said, and I raced out the door, wondering what was going on at Mark's house.

32

I banged on Mark's door, but there was no answer. I rang the doorbell. I pounded on the door again.

Still, no one came to the door.

I ran around back, thinking maybe Mark was in the backyard. There was no one there.

I raced back around to the front of the house. My worry and fear grew.

Mark should be home, I thought. *When I left the toy store, he said he was headed right for his house. He should be here.*

Then, another thought occurred to me.

Maybe he is here. Maybe someone—or something—won't let him come to the door.

The monkey.

Again, I pounded on the door.

"Mark!" I shouted. "Are you home?!?!"

I stepped to the side of the porch and peered through the living room window. What I saw made my blood freeze.

In the living room, Mark and his mom were sitting cross-legged on the floor. Their arms were spread wide, and they were slapping their hands together, like they were banging cymbals. The monkey sat on a recliner, facing them. He, too, was flailing his arms. His eyes blinked red, and he looked mean. The tiny cymbals in his paws crashed together, but, being outside, I couldn't hear them.

"Mark!" I shouted, trying to get his attention. *"Mark!"*

Neither he nor his mother paid any attention to me. The monkey had them under his spell.

I pounded on the door again and tried the knob. It turned, and I pushed the door open and stepped inside.

"Mark!" I shouted again. *"Mrs. Bruder!"*

Still, they paid no attention to me. It was like I wasn't even there! They just sat on the floor, watching the monkey, slapping their hands together like they were banging cymbals, imitating the monkey.

Enough of this, I thought. In three giant steps, I was at the recliner. I reached down to grab the toy and pull out the batteries . . . but the monkey had other ideas.

When I reached down to grab the monkey, the crazy thing turned and slapped the cymbals around one of my fingers! Now, I know they were only small cymbals, and the monkey was only twelve inches tall . . . but it *hurt!* Then, he bit my finger . . . and that hurt even *worse!*

I yelped and pulled my hand away, and the monkey came with it. He had his cymbals and teeth firmly planted around my fingers, and he wasn't letting go.

On the floor, Mark and his mom continued slapping their hands together. They had dazed looks in their eyes. They probably didn't even know I was in their house!

The monkey continued to bite down on my fingers. I swung him around, up and over my head, and finally succeeded in getting free. He lost his grip and went sailing into the far wall. He hit a picture frame and it crashed to the floor, but, amazingly, it didn't break.

But the monkey wasn't through. He ran toward me, banging his cymbals and snapping his jaws . . . but there was no way I was going to let him bite me again!

So, I drew my right leg back and gave him a good, hard, swift kick. My shoe connected, and the monkey went flying into the air and out the front door.

On the floor, Mark and his mom continued slapping their hands together. They weren't in any immediate danger, so I left them and ran out the front door.

Already, the monkey had regained himself and was readying for another attack. But I struck first, and I ran to where he was in the grass and gave him another hard kick. He sailed through the air like a football, higher and higher . . . and dropped down in the middle of the street. I chased after him, but I stopped at the curb . . . just as a passing car ran over the toy! There was a crunching sound as the wheels went over the monkey. The car slowed and pulled to the side of the road, but I barely noticed. I was focused on the monkey. Actually, I expected the thing to get up and come after me again.

But I wasn't going to give him the chance. I made sure there were no cars coming, then I walked into the street. I carefully picked up what was left of the toy, found his battery compartment in his leg, and took out the single red battery.

It was over.

I walked to the curb, carrying the monkey. The man who had been driving the car hurried up to me.

"I'm really sorry I ran over your toy," he said. "I didn't see it until the very last second. It was like it came out of nowhere."

I shrugged. "It's okay," I said. "I didn't like this toy, anyway."

The man apologized again before walking back to his car and driving off.

Behind me, I heard Mark call out. "Hey, Eric!" he exclaimed. "When did you get here?"

I looked at the crushed monkey in my hands, and all I could do was laugh. Our ordeal was over.

Or . . . was it?

Mark's mom had no memory of what had happened. She made no mention of anything, except for the comment she made wondering why the picture frame was on the floor. Of course, I explained everything to Mark later. He, too, had no memory of sitting cross-legged on the floor, slapping his hands together, imitating the monkey.

"You should have seen yourself," I said. "You looked pretty silly. And your mom looked even sillier."

Mark laughed and shook his head. "I'm glad this whole thing is over," he said.

"Yeah, me, too," I replied.

Remembering my promise to Mom, I said good-bye to Mark and sprinted home. Before I mowed the lawn, I called Shayleen, just to make sure she'd made it home okay. She said she had, after she'd helped Mr. Kleagle clean up the mess.

It took me about an hour to mow the lawn, and then I went inside for lunch. Madeline was seated on the couch, reading a book out loud to her doll.

"So, what have you been up to all morning, besides mowing the lawn?" Mom asked.

"You wouldn't believe me if I told you," I said.

"Try me," Mom said, sitting down at the dining room table.

"Well, we went down to the new toy store to take a look inside before it opens," I said. "All of the toys came to life and attacked us. But we were able to get the batteries out of all of them, and it won't happen again. When I came home, you and Madeline were under Priscilla's power, but I was able to get her batteries out. We're all lucky to be alive."

"I see," Mom said with a wide smile. "Toys

that come to life, huh? Eric . . . I just don't know where you come up with this stuff."

"I said you wouldn't believe me," I said, taking a bite of my sandwich.

"Oh, I believe you," Mom said. "I believe you have a very active imagination, and that's good."

After I finished lunch, I gathered up my fishing gear and headed over to Shayleen's house. She retrieved her fishing pole and bucket from the garage, and we hiked over to Mark's. While we walked, I told her all about what had happened with Priscilla and with Mark's monkey.

"You guys were both really lucky," she said.

"We all were," I replied. "But we don't have anything to worry about anymore."

When we reached Mark's house, their car was gone. Still, I banged on the front door to see if anyone was home. Nope.

"Looks like you and I are going to be the only ones fishing today," I said. "Mark's not home."

We headed out, and, of course, we'd have to pass by the toy store on our way . . . and we were in for yet another surprise.

There was a big sign in the window that read: *NOW OPEN!*

"I can't believe it!" I said. "After what happened this morning, I can't believe the store is open so fast!"

"I helped him clean up," Shayleen said, "but I didn't think he'd be open so soon. Let's go inside!"

We walked up to the front door. I pushed it open, and we went in.

The toys were all in their places, and everything had been cleaned up. The dolls stood straight, the toy soldiers stood at attention. The stuffed animals were once again piled in the corner. Model airplanes and rockets hung from the ceiling. But Mr. Kleagle was nowhere to be found.

"It's like nothing even happened," Shayleen whispered.

Right at that moment, a movement on the far side of the store caught my attention. I turned.

A doll was walking toward us! She had come to life again and was stumbling toward us! Our nightmare wasn't over, after all!

Shayleen and I were just about to turn and run, when Mr. Kleagle appeared from a back room. I pointed at the doll.

"Mr. Kleagle!" I shouted. *"We missed one!"*

Mr. Kleagle gave me a puzzled look. He glanced at the doll, then he laughed. "Oh, no, not at all," he said, walking over to the doll. He picked her up, but she continued to move her legs forward and backward. "I've replaced the batteries in all of my toys. This time, however, I used *real* batteries and not my experimental ones."

That's a relief, I thought.

"I can't believe you've opened the store so

soon," Shayleen said.

"I decided not to wait for the weekend," Mr. Kleagle said. "Very few toys were broken. All I had to do was put batteries in all of them."

While we were talking to Mr. Kleagle, a family came in. Their two children gasped in awe as they looked around.

"Welcome, friends!" Mr. Kleagle said to them. "Have a look around. You'll find some of the most amazing toys in the world! If you have any questions, just ask!"

The family fanned out, and their two children giggled with delight as they looked at all of Mr. Kleagle's toys.

"In all of the confusion," Mr. Kleagle said to Shayleen and me, "I forgot to thank you for your help today. I had no idea my toys could get so out of hand. It was a lesson well-learned, and I'm glad no one was hurt."

"We're glad, too," I said. "We'll visit often, now that we know we're not going to be attacked by toys."

We said good-bye and headed for the pond. There, Shayleen gave me some bad news. We were sitting on the riverbank. The sky had cleared, and the sun had come out. We weren't catching any fish, so we talked a lot.

"We're moving away," she said.

I was stunned. I'd known Shayleen all my life.

"Moving away?!?!" I exclaimed. "Why? When?"

"My dad took a job in New Jersey," she explained. "We're moving in two weeks."

Those two weeks were really hard, and saying good-bye to Shayleen was the hardest thing I'd ever done. We planned to write and to call, but it still wouldn't be the same. I received a letter from her a week after she'd moved. She said they moved to a city in New Jersey called Medford, and she'd already met some new friends. I wrote her back, and we exchanged a few more letters over the next few months. I called her on her birthday in November, but, after that, we didn't write very much. In fact, the last time I got a letter from her was in January. Months rolled past, and, while I never forgot about her, I didn't think about her as much. I guess that's just the way things go, sometimes. Time passes, and things change.

Then, in July, months after I'd last heard from her, she called me on the phone. It was great to talk to her. She said she liked school, but she was on summer break, and she and her family had recently returned from a vacation at the ocean.

"It was the worst vacation ever!" Shayleen said.

"Why?" I asked. "What happened?"

"Remember the trouble we had with the toys and the toy store?" she asked.

"How can I forget?" I replied. "Every time I see a toy, it reminds me of what happened."

"Well, our vacation was worse," Shayleen said.

"Worse?" I said. "How can anything be worse than toys that come to life and have a mind of their own?"

"Oh, those toys were bad, all right," Shayleen said. "But they were nothing like nuclear jellyfish."

"Nuclear jellyfish?!?!" I exclaimed. "What are you talking about?!?!"

"It was a nightmare," Shayleen said. "Want

to hear about what happened?"

"Are you kidding?!?!" I said, nearly shouting.

"It all started at the beach," Shayleen began, and I held the phone to my ear for nearly an hour as she told me all about her experience with the horrifying nuclear jellyfish of New Jersey . . . .

Next:

**#22: Nuclear
Jellyfish
of
New Jersey**

**Continue on for
a FREE preview!**

At first, I didn't like New Jersey. Oh, there's nothing wrong with the state at all, and now I love it here. But my family moved here from Tennessee, and I had to leave all my friends behind. That was really, really hard.

My name is Shayleen Mills, and I live in Medford, New Jersey. We moved here last summer, when my dad took a job here. I didn't want to leave Tennessee, but soon, I made a bunch of new friends.

And now I like New Jersey. It's a lot

different from Tennessee. I can't say I like one state better than the other. It's hard to compare the two, because there are so many cool things about both states.

I can say, however, there is one thing I don't like about Tennessee: toys and toy stores. Earlier this summer, my friends Eric Carter and Mark Bruder had a really freaky thing happen to us, and it had to do with toys that came to life. It was really scary . . . but that's another story altogether.

And, if you want to know the truth, there's something I don't like about New Jersey:

The ocean.

Now, I know what you're probably thinking. You're thinking that I can't swim, or I don't like salt water. You're thinking that maybe I don't like the hot sun or the sandy beaches. Wrong. I love it all.

It's what's *in* the ocean that I don't like, and I'm not talking about sharks or barracuda or killer whales. I'm talking about something that's totally different . . . something that no one even knew existed, until this summer.

Jellyfish.

Now, jellyfish alone can be bad enough. The sting of a jellyfish can be very painful. Sometimes, they can be fatal.

But, I'm not talking about plain old jellyfish. I'm talking about radioactive creatures—nuclear jellyfish—that are far, far more dangerous than normal jellyfish. And if I thought my ordeal with terrifying toys was bad, it couldn't compare with the horrors that my family and friends went through in a small vacation town on the east coast of New Jersey.

We moved from Murfreesboro, Tennessee, to Medford, New Jersey, in the middle of summer. It took us a few days to get settled in to our new home, because we had a lot of things to unpack. In fact, for a few days, the only things I had in my bedroom were my bed, a chair, and a few boxes of clothing.

But we finally got everything unpacked and put away, and I arranged everything in my room just like it had been at our old home in Tennessee. I have a baby brother named Lee, and I helped him arrange his room. Actually, I was the only one who did the arranging. He just played around, mostly. Lee is only two years old, but he manages to get into all sorts of trouble. He's really curious, and he's always poking around where he shouldn't be. We have to keep an eye on him all the time so he doesn't do something to hurt himself. Sure, he doesn't *mean* to get into trouble . . . but he's only two and he doesn't know any better.

I, however, am a lot older, and I *should* know better. Usually, I can spot trouble coming a mile away. In fact, I knew there was something strange about that toy store in Tennessee. And I knew that the toys meant trouble.

But how was I to know about the trouble that was coming when we went on a short, weekend vacation to the New Jersey coast? How was I supposed to know the four days we spent in Wildwood, a popular tourist destination in southeastern New Jersey, would be a disaster?

We had only been in our new home in Medford for about a month when Dad suggested we take a short vacation. He'd been working long days at his new job. He said he had to, because there was a lot of new things to learn. But he said he needed a break, and decided we should take a short vacation. Not just a vacation, but a trip to the Atlantic Ocean!

That would be awesome! I hadn't been anywhere else in New Jersey except Medford. In fact, I've never even seen the ocean before! I couldn't wait to wade and swim and splash in the waves. I couldn't wait to hear the roar of the surf and seagulls crying out overhead.

Mom, Lee and I went shopping the day before we left. We bought some new towels and a big beach umbrella, and I got a new bathing suit. Mom also bought Lee a plastic pail and a few plastic shovels so he could play in the sand.

And the next day, when we arrived in Wildwood, I couldn't believe it! It had the coolest amusement park I'd ever seen in my life! Dad had told me all about it, but I never imagined it would be so big. We drove by a place called the Boardwalk, where I saw a huge, twisting roller coaster, a gigantic Ferris wheel, and lots more rides. There were gobs and gobs of people all over the place! The sun was shining, the surf was pounding, and there were lots of people swimming.

"This is incredible!" I said, nearly shouting from the back seat of the car.

"I thought you'd like it," Dad said. "And the weather is supposed to be hot and sunny the whole time we're here. After we check in to our hotel, we'll relax on the beach for while before we go sightseeing. I think we're all going to have a great time."

Now, my dad is almost always right about *everything*. He's one of the smartest dads in the world, in my opinion.

But this time, he was wrong. Sure, we all started out having a great time, but it wasn't long before things went very wrong . . . only moments after I'd waded into the ocean.

We found our hotel, which was right on the beach. It was so cool! We were on the second floor, and there was a sliding glass door and a deck right off our room. There was a small table and a few chairs on the deck, if we wanted to eat outside or just relax. Mom slid open the glass panel door, and the room was suddenly awash with warm ocean air. Below, on the beach, there were people everywhere! Colorful beach towels and umbrellas dotted the white sand. People walked along the shore and swam in the water. Several people were trying to surf, but it didn't look like the waves were big enough.

"Rides! Rides!" Lee squealed as he looked at the amusement park in the distance. He was excited, too, but he wasn't big enough to go on most of the rides. Still, I knew he would have a lot of fun.

"Let's get unpacked so we can go the beach!" I said, turning and walking back into the hotel room. Mom and Lee followed.

"I'll bet we'll see some beautiful sunrises," Dad said as we unpacked our clothes and put them in the dresser.

"You will," Mom smirked. "We're on vacation. I'm planning on sleeping late."

We changed into our swimsuits, and it wasn't very long before we were ready to go. Mom packed a beach bag with towels, some bottled water, snacks, and Lee's plastic pail and shovels. She handed me a bottle of sun screen.

"Shayleen, can you take care of your brother?" she asked.

"Sure," I said.

"And make sure you get enough for

yourself."

"Gotcha," I replied. "Lee . . . come here."

Lee was standing by the open sliding glass door, looking out. When I called him, he walked over to me.

"I've got to put this sun screen on you, okay?" I said. "Don't make a fuss like last time."

Before we'd moved, Mom and Lee and I went to the beach. Mom asked me to put sun screen on Lee, but he was so freaked out that he ran off! I didn't know what his problem was. It was just sun screen. I had to chase him all over the beach, catch him, and take him back to the picnic area. He'd even started crying!

Lee shook his head as I opened the bottle. "No, no, no," he said.

And that's when Mom stepped in. "Lee," she said sternly, "if you don't let your sister put sun screen on you, you're staying in the hotel room."

Lee looked at Mom, and I could tell he got the message. He didn't fuss a bit as I rubbed sun screen all over him.

"There," I said. "All done."

After I covered my exposed skin with sun

screen, I handed the bottle back to Mom. Dad had gone to get a bucket of ice, and he returned.

"You guys all set?" he asked.

"Yeah!" I said. "Let's go to the beach!"

"Beach! Beach! Beach!" Lee exclaimed. He bounced up and down like a kangaroo.

We took the stairs down, and came out on the beach. Again, I was hit by warm, salty air. The sand was hot beneath my feet, but I didn't mind.

And we get to spend four whole days here! I thought. *What fun!*

We found a place on the beach, and Mom and Dad spread out a blanket. Dad opened up the umbrella. It was huge! He positioned it so we could sit in its shade, out of the burning rays of the sun.

But I wasn't sitting around! I wanted to be in the water!

"Let's go swimming!" I said.

"I'll take you and Lee down to the shore," Dad said.

"I'm going to stay right here and read, Mom said, and she reached into her bag and pulled out a book. "You guys have fun."

Dad, Lee, and I held hands as we walked toward the ocean, skirting around dozens of people sitting or lying on blankets. Some kids were playing catch with a football, and I saw a few kites in the air. Seagulls whirled above, gracefully gliding on currents of air.

When we reached the water, I let go of Dad's hand.

"Remember what I told you," he said. "Don't go in farther than your waist. The ocean is very different than the lakes and pools you've been in. The currents here can be really strong. We don't want you pulled out to sea and eaten by a killer whale."

"Dad," I said, rolling my eyes. *Killer whales,* I thought. *Right.*

He laughed and sat down in the sand. Lee was carrying his pail and a blue plastic shovel, and he knelt down and started to dig. Just what he was digging for, I didn't know. But it looked like he was having fun.

I waded into the water. The surf came splashed up to my knees. The water was cool and refreshing. Then, it reversed itself, and receded back. I was standing in ankle-deep water.

I continued walking out into the water. There were people all around, talking, laughing, splashing, and playing. Everyone was having just as much fun as I was!

But there was also something else around.

Something I'd only seen on television and movies.

A shark.

It was coming right at me, but by the time I saw the dorsal fin emerge from the water, it was only a few feet away . . . and there was no way I could escape.

ABOUT THE AUTHOR

Johnathan Rand is the author of more than 50 books, with well over 2 million copies in print. Series include **AMERICAN CHILLERS, MICHIGAN CHILLERS, FREDDIE FERNORTNER, FEARLESS FIRST GRADER,** and **THE ADVENTURE CLUB.** He's also co-authored a novel for teens (with Christopher Knight) entitled **PANDEMIA.** When not traveling, Rand lives in northern Michigan with his wife and two dogs. He is also the only author in the world to have a store that sells only his works: **CHILLERMANIA!** is located in Indian River, Michigan. Johnathan Rand is not always at the store, but he has been known to drop by frequently. Find out more at:

www.americanchillers.com

FUN FACTS ABOUT TENNESSEE:

State Capital: Nashville

Largest City: Memphis

Statehood: June 1st, 1796 (16th state)

State Nickname: The Volunteer State

State Reptile: Eastern Box Turtle

State Amphibian: Tennessee Cave Salamander

State Butterfly: Zebra Swallowtail

State Animal: Raccoon

State Bird: Mockingbird

State Flower: Iris

State Tree: Tulip Poplar

State Gem: Tennessee River Pearl

FAMOUS TENNESSEEANS:

John Agee - Novelist/Journalist/Screenwriter

Dolly Parton - Singer/Actress

Davy Crockett - Frontiersman/Soldier/Folk Hero

Tina Turner - Singer

Morgan Freeman - Actor

Aretha Franklin - Singer

Lester Flatt - Musician

Cybill Shepherd - Actress

Tennessee Ernie Ford - Singer

Isaac Hayes - Composer

Sequoia - Cherokee Scholar/Educator

among many, many more!

Join the official

AMERICAN

CHILLERS

FAN CLUB!

Visit www.americanchillers.com for details!

Also by Johnathan Rand:

GHOST IN THE GRAVEYARD

Johnathan Rand travels internationally for school visits and book signings! For booking information, call:

1 (231) 238-0338!

www.americanchillers.com

All AudioCraft books are proudly printed, bound, and manufactured in the United States of America, utilizing American resources, labor, and materials.

USA